T0114995

THE
SUPPORT
GROUP

A MYSTERY NOVEL

DONNA REUTZEL UNDERWOOD

abbott press®

A DIVISION OF WRITER'S DIGEST

Copyright © 2014 Donna Reutzel Underwood.

All rights reserved. No part of this book may be used or reproduced by
any means, graphic, electronic, or mechanical, including photocopying,
recording, taping or by any information storage retrieval system
without the written permission of the publisher except in the case
of brief quotations embodied in critical articles and reviews.

This is a work of fiction. All of the characters, names, incidents,
organizations, and dialogue in this novel are either the products
of the author's imagination or are used fictitiously.

Abbott Press books may be ordered through booksellers or by contacting:

Abbott Press
1663 Liberty Drive
Bloomington, IN 47403
www.abbottpress.com
Phone: 1-866-697-5310

Because of the dynamic nature of the Internet, any web addresses or
links contained in this book may have changed since publication and
may no longer be valid. The views expressed in this work are solely those
of the author and do not necessarily reflect the views of the publisher,
and the publisher hereby disclaims any responsibility for them.

Any people depicted in stock imagery provided by Thinkstock are models,
and such images are being used for illustrative purposes only.
Certain stock imagery © Thinkstock.

ISBN: 978-1-4582-1567-3 (sc)
ISBN: 978-1-4582-1569-7 (hc)
ISBN: 978-1-4582-1568-0 (e)

Library of Congress Control Number: 2014907682

Printed in the United States of America.

Abbott Press rev. date: 5/6/2014

DEDICATED...

To everyone who has buried a loved one.

"What we once enjoyed and deeply loved we can never lose, for all that we love deeply becomes part of us."

Helen Keller

MY DEEPEST GRATITUDE TO:

My husband, Wayne, for his loving patience, encouragement, and for loving me.

My friends, Paula Vedder, Melanie Smith, and Rosann Ferris for their willingness to read the manuscript, more than one time, and add helpful suggestions.

Joy Johnson, co-founder of the Centering Corporation.

Stu Burns, Kaitlyn Hayes, Kayla Engelhaupt, and Marcia Calhoun Forecki for their editing skills.

OTHER BOOKS BY THE AUTHOR:

Original Loss

Grief Works

Original Loss Revisited

CHAPTER I

The Circumstances of a Death Affect the Grief Work

MONDAY

Brooksie sits at her desk for over an hour watching the sun retreat behind the mountains. She tries to absorb what she just finished reading in today's newspaper about the death of a Mr. Ray Sorensen. He was a client in a grief group only half a year ago. His wife had drowned earlier and he was struggling with his loss. She was one of the facilitators in his group.

A loud banging on her door nearly causes her to drop her coffee cup.

"Come in before you knock down the door!" Brooksie yells.

Lucinda, another facilitator, races in and throws a newspaper on the desk. "Did you see the article about the death of Ray Sorenson? The police are saying his death is being investigated as a possible homicide. You and I were facilitators in his group. I've never known anyone who was murdered before. It seems surreal and gives me the creeps."

"I just finished reading the article," says Brooksie. "I feel heartsick for Ray's young daughter, who is now an orphan. I can't imagine how a young child copes with a double tragedy. Children don't have the words to describe their feelings, especially when the feelings are all over the map. I remember Ray was in a widower's group because his wife had been sucked into the selfish arms of Lake Winsome and drowned just six months before he joined the group. It sounds as if the police aren't sure how he died. The article states possible homicide."

Lucinda goes on to reread aloud the information given in the paper. "Sorenson's sailboat was found about five miles outside the harbor with no one on board and the dingy missing. There is speculation, but nothing concrete, that there may have been another person present. Only one body has been recovered, and the coast guard is continuing the search for another person or persons. Sorensen was first thought to have drowned, but the autopsy has not been completed. Foul play has not been ruled out."

"You, Virginia, and I were the facilitators for the group. Have you ever known anyone personally who was murdered?"

"Yes," Brooksie answers. "My neighbor's twenty-five year old daughter was brutally murdered. She was kidnapped by a stranger, raped, and tortured for days, finally killed and her mutilated body thrown in a dumpster. Eventually, the scum bag was caught. Then the legal system caused even more upheaval for her family, because it took years to find the bastard guilty and finally sentence him to life behind bars. The lawyers filed several appeals which prolonged the process even more. My stomach churns every time I remember the cruelty, fear, and pain the young woman endured for many days, and the continuing anguish of the family."

Later that day, Brooksie calls Ray Sorensen's home and a soft spoken woman answers. After Brooksie introduces herself, the lady tells her she is Macy's grandmother and Ray's mother.

Brooksie says, "I am so very sorry about the loss of your son and that Macy has lost both parents. I can't imagine how difficult Ray's death must be for the two of you."

Mrs. Sorensen asks if it would be possible for a counselor to come to the house to visit with the two of them. She expresses concern for her granddaughter. A date and time is set for the requested visit.

Brooksie thinks to herself. *I wonder how they are communicating their feelings to each other, since there is such an age spread between them, as well as different life experiences. The grief work for both of them is complicated, because of the way Ray and his wife died. A sudden, violent death is traumatic for those left behind and can prolong the length of mourning. Macy has lost a mother who drowned and a father who has possibly been murdered! God, I hope their deaths are not connected.*

The ringing of the phone interrupts her thoughts. "Hello? Oh, hi, Aunt Tilly. What's up?

"I just wanted to give you a heads-up. I'm dropping by your house later today to leave you, temporarily, a very special and needy cat. I know how partial you are to yellow felines and this one is truly one of a kind."

"Not this time my dear aunt. I don't have room for a homeless yellow cat," says Brooksie pleadingly. Please don't start with the guilt routine. I'm sure he's a fantastic cat, and I know you will find him a loving home, just not with me."

"Now Brooksie," says Aunt Tilly, "you only need to take care of this old precious cat for a short time. He probably doesn't have much time left on this planet anyway. I know by tomorrow or the next day I will find some caring person who will give Samson a permanent home, if you would just foster the little guy for a few days. Samson is so sweet and no trouble at all."

"You've already given him a name?" says Brooksie. "You're devious and have no scruples. You know darn well that you are not asking me to foster this cat. You have no intention of finding him another home. If I give in and take him on a pretend temporary placement, you know I'll have six cats."

"Now dear, I'll just drop by this evening and let you have a look-see at Samson. 'Bye for now."

"Don't hang up, Auntie!" The phone is dead. *Damn. She's impossible! I could pretend not to be at home when she comes by, but that never works. She has a key, and isn't shy about using it.*

Brooksie continues, *I need to stop dwelling on Aunt Tilly and Samson, who will soon be living with me. I want to focus on what I remember of Ray Sorensen from the twelve weeks he attended the grief group. He seemed devoted to his daughter and had apparently been very happy with his wife. As a family, they spent much of their free time in sports activities. He and his wife loved to dance. I remember him saying one time, 'Losing my wife has made me feel like an amputee, a part of me has been cut off. I have been cut off at the knees. No more dancing.'*

Brooksie makes a beeline for the filing cabinet to get Sorensen's chart. She comes across a note written by Lucinda. She wrote as the sessions neared the end, that he shared with the group that he had met a very nice lady and that they had a "coffee date." Ray said something about her being a great listener. She even loved the water like he did. He also mentioned something about a problem brewing with his daughter resenting his new lady friend. He was troubled by his daughter's attitude and hurt feelings, but he seemed quite pleased with his budding relationship.

Brooksie decides she is to be the one to visit with Ray's mother and daughter, since Lucinda already has other plans and Virginia isn't a counselor. *God, I hope this crime, if it is one, can be quickly solved by the police.* Brooksie's thoughts are again interrupted by Melissa, "You have a call, someone from the police department".

"Hello. Brooksie Everett speaking."

"Hello Ms. Everett, this is Detective Blake Marino of the Whitefall Police Department. Do you have a moment to answer a few questions? Your secretary thought you might be the person I should talk with. I am inquiring about a former client, a Mr. Ray Sorensen."

"What is it you want to know?" Brooksie asks.

Detective Marino answers, "Have you read this morning's paper about Mr. Sorensen?"

"Yes," says Brooksie. "What a shock and what a double tragedy for his family. Are you still considering his death a possible homicide?"

"Not able to answer your question at this time," responds Detective Marino. "My partner and I would like to visit your office and speak with the staff about Mr. Sorensen. Could we set a date for today? Is there a time that would be convenient?"

Brooksie answers, "You do understand we have confidentiality issues?"

The detective says, "Yes, we are aware of this. We will certainly respect confidentiality, but at this time we are conducting an investigation and cooperation will be expected and appreciated."

Brooksie repeats, "I can't guarantee everyone will be available, but I'll do my best to get the staff together today at 5:00 p.m."

"I'll be there with my partner, Detective Swain. If you have any other questions after we meet then feel free to call me," responds Detective Marino. He leaves his number and thanks her for her cooperation.

Brooksie asks Melissa to telephone Virginia and see if she can make it to the office at 5:00 p.m.

"I will inform Lucinda about the meeting," says Brooksie. "Melissa you also need to attend."

"I can't believe that someone would murder Mr. Sorensen. He was a good looking man and was getting on with his life. He was always so polite to me. What a waste," says Melissa. "Do you need me to do anything else?"

"No," Brooksie answers. "Not at this time. The detectives will tell us what they need. Second thought, maybe you could have some coffee and snacks brought from the deli. We all know how cranky Lucinda gets on an empty stomach."

"Consider it done."

CHAPTER II

Grief is Immeasurable and Individual

SESSION ONE
GETTING ACQUAINTED

It is time for the next group to begin. Rachael and Anita are organizing things. Anita plugs in the coffee pots, one regular and the other unleaded. She informs Rachael and Brooksie, in her sweet voice, that she has brought a variety of fruit. "Mourners really need healthy snacks because half of the time they forget to eat or just can't." Anita is close to twenty six years of age, and works hard to please everyone. This habit of trying to please everyone is a throw back from the time she and her brother lived with her cold and critical aunt.

Soon, the group members trickle in one and two at a time. Rachael greets them at the door, and hands them name tags. Rachael is in amazing shape. She hikes, sails, and loves to water ski and snow ski. She is very pretty and looks younger than her thirty-three years. Just like most of the staff, she has lost loved ones. Her mother died when she was ten years old, and she was raised by her dad. She tells it, that is, when she is actually willing to talk about the past. She left home at the age of seventeen because she couldn't get along with her stepmother. She married at age eighteen and was divorced by the time she was twenty. She is definitely an excellent advocate for abused children and very vocal about her passion for holding the abusive parents accountable.

The first session is always the most difficult for the newcomers. The facilitators try to make the surroundings as comfortable and welcoming as possible, but it always feels more like a funeral parlor, minus the usual, large displays of flower arrangements.

Recollections leap from Brooksie's memory bank, *I can vividly remember the first time I attended such a group.* She thinks to herself. *Even though it was much overdue, years after my losses, I can still feel the choking sensation. There didn't seem to be enough air in the room. It felt like a tidal wave was approaching and I wanted to run away as fast as I could. Death by drowning was only seconds away. I needed to run like the wind, but my legs wouldn't move. I have a memory of those terrifying sensations deep within my cells. It felt like my feet were held tight by a large sea-going ship's anchor. I could see an enormous wave, tall as a skyscraper, moving in slow motion toward me. I was paralyzed, helplessly watching death approach me. I don't think I can ever have enough trust or courage to love again, except for pets.*

The three facilitators greet each individual by shaking their hand. Eye contact is infrequent, but a few try. The eyelids of a few appear swollen and raw, from the constant wiping away of tears. An unspoken sorrow quickly and silently passes through the room. You can almost hear some of their thoughts: *I don't belong here. I want to turn around and run out the door. This can't be real.* Some let their tears flow down without restraint. A few appear slightly relieved, as if maybe they could finally find comfort and hope in this room of strangers.

The facilitators instruct the members to find a seat. Slowly, they pick one and quietly sit down. Most have their eyes cast downward. Introductions are made by Anita as she a passes out index cards and pencils to each one and tells them, "Please take a few minutes and briefly write down some specifics about the death of your loved one. For example, how, when, and why they died, their age, and how long you were in each others' lives.

When you finish writing, please pass your card to the person on your right."

"Experience has shown us that it is easier to tell someone else's story in the first session," says Rachael.

Before a person is asked to read their neighbor's card, Rachael reminds the mourners that what is said in group needs to remain in group. No names or stories with specifics are to be shared outside the group. It is important for all to feel that what they say will be respected and kept private so that everyone can feel safe being honest.

After five minutes pass, Anita asks for a volunteer who would be willing to read the card they receive from their neighbor, to the left of them. "Please give your own name and the name on the card," she instructs.

Mary hesitantly raises her ample arm and gives her name. "I am Mary and I will read Marshall's card." She takes a breath and begins, "My partner of ten years, Thom, died in a car accident eleven months ago. The driver of the other car was drunk. Thom lingered in critical condition for two days and finally died. Every day and every minute is a struggle for me. I can hardly catch my breath." Mary places the card in her lap and timidly looks at Harvey.

Without hesitating, Harvey states his name and says, "I have Mary's card. She writes, 'Sam, my husband of thirty-five years, died from a heart attack. There was no time for goodbye."

Kathy is next in the circle and she reads Harvey's card. "My wife's name was Helen. She was forty-two and died of cancer. She was very sick for eighteen months. We were married for twenty years and have a nineteen year old son."

Justin, after adjusting his glasses, reads Kathy's card. "Dick was my husband for five years, but we were actually together for ten. He was murdered six weeks ago by two would-be thieves. They shot him and he died instantly."

Kathy sighs and adds in a barely perceptible voice, "If he

hadn't tried to be a hero he would be alive today and I wouldn't be sitting in this room."

Heidi with a flushed face and swollen red eyelids, reads Justin's card. "My wife died of cancer. Her name was Marinda and she was forty-nine. She was diagnosed with ovarian cancer only twelve months before her death. We had been married for thirty years. She left me with a teenage daughter living at home and another son and daughter who have their own families."

Dell's voice cracks. Pausing, he reads from Heidi's card held in his unsteady hand. "My fiancé killed himself with a gun six months ago. We were to be married two weeks from today." Heidi's eyes look like two burned out sockets, and both fists are clenched. Not once did she look at anyone in the room. Her eyes fill to the brim with tears, but she keeps taking deep breaths, apparently attempting to keep herself under control.

Marshall reads Dell's card. "My wife Marcia, only thirty-two years old, fell over a cliff and died. We had been married for thirteen years. She was trying to take a picture of my daughter and myself when she tripped and fell."

This part of the first session is deeply emotional, not only for the clients, but also for the facilitators.

Justin adds, "I am not sure that this kind of group is right for me. This clinic was recommended to me by a colleague, Dr. Leek."

"This is your decision, Justin, but we do advise everyone to give themselves a chance for one or two sessions," offers Rachael.

There is a pause that gently passes through the group.

Justin is the first one to volunteer information about himself. He speaks of his children, two daughters, and one son. He says the oldest is thirty and the youngest is sixteen.

"The sixteen year old girl lives at home. I am an M.D. and my specialty is orthopedics. My favorite hobbies are skiing and traveling. I'm often accused of drumming up business on the slopes for my practice." He glances over at Dell and says,

"I don't know how to be a mother to a young girl. My wife was the nurturer. I have never been really close to either daughter. Guess I have been more comfortable relating to my wife and son. Marinda was such a great mother."

Justin continues, "My own parents were fairly distant from me and my brother. They never attended any of our school functions, nor showed any interest in anything we did. They took many so-called business trips and left us with a nanny and a housekeeper. I guess we both turned out okay because we have good careers. Marinda was the opposite of my mother. My wife demonstrated her love for me and the children on a daily basis. I can't remember my mother ever hugging me or my brother." Again, he looks over at Dell.

"Justin, it isn't so hard to be a dad," offers Dell. "It is not true that women are the only ones who can nurture. I just try to have fun with my daughter. When I don't know what to say to her, I ask my mother-in-law to take over. My hobbies are sailing and other water sports. Before my wife died, we both enjoyed sailing our boat. My daughter, Cherish, is eleven and she also loves the same sports. Now, it is just the two of us trying to enjoy the water again. It's hard at times. She has always been a daddy's girl, at the same time quite self-sufficient. Now she's very anxious and clings to me. She even asks me if I really have to go to work. I wonder if she worries about me dying?" He pauses and looks into the distance.

Mary speaks next. "I am an RN and have been working for over fifteen years. I'm also a house wife. Well, I guess now I just take care of the house; I'm no longer a wife. Widow is such a lonely word. I have four grown children all into their own lives now. I feel left behind in a big, empty house." Tears roll down her cheeks and onto her long, plaid skirt. She raises a much used handkerchief to brush them aside.

"I was brought up to be strong and to keep my emotions in

check. It has always been expected of me to stay calm, no matter what the circumstances." Justin's voice cracks.

"Well, I'm a doctor, for Christ sake. I can't fall apart at every crisis. What kind of doctor cries in front of his patients?" says Justin in a loud voice.

Heidi responds first, "A compassionate, honest one does. I would love to find a doctor who shares his feelings. By the way, just because you have a high paying job doesn't make you a successful person. We should be judged by our behaviors, not by our bank account."

Rachael gently intervenes and asks Heidi if she would be comfortable sharing something about herself to help the group to get to know her a little better.

"I want to feel like I did before my fiancé died." Heidi answers in an angry tone. "I want to know that I will once again feel joy, laughter, and hope. I want to know this pain in my heart and head will go away, and I want to know when. If I have to feel the way I have for the past six months, I don't want to be alive." Heidi sinks down into her chair covering her face with her hands.

Rachel asks Heidi if she feels like taking her own life.

Heidi practically whispers her response, "Not really, but I do think it would be much easier if I could just drop dead, maybe if my heart would just stop beating or if I would be hit by a car and die instantly."

Two others in the group speak of just wanting to go to sleep and not wake up. They say they have not made any kind of plans to cause themselves harm, but simply want relief from this awful, unending anguish and longing.

At this point a short break is suggested. "Restrooms are to your left and we have some refreshments at the back of the room," announces Anita.

After the break, the group work continues. There is intermittent sharing by most. Justin is the most verbal, but he is not able to get in touch with his feelings. This is not a surprise since he received so little affection from his parents. Heidi remains silent for the last hour, but does appear to be listening to the others. Her anger seems more directed at the facilitators, rather than at the bereaved members.

Brooksie tells the group, "There is healing power in being able to tell one's story, in any kind of voice that feelings permit, whether angry, mournful, loud, or whispered. Healthy expression is the key to finding compassion for others and for oneself."

The group ends after two hours, and a few remain to chat or ask questions. When only the facilitators are left, they do their usual rehashing of what they heard, observed, and any concerns about group members. They talk about their personal emotions that may have arisen during the session. The three agree that these seven people are unwilling mourners. For some, the deaths were sudden. For others, there was a little more time since their loved ones died of illnesses. Uninvited death has shaken their world off of its foundation and each one is, in their own unique way, attempting to make sense of the loss that has befallen them. This role of widow and widower was given to them without their permission or request. After sharing their common concern about Heidi and her anger, Rachael offers to call her tomorrow to let her know that the staff care about her and are available twenty-four seven.

The conversation then turns to the death of Ray Sorensen. Discussion about what is remembered of him and concerns for the family now left behind. After awhile, the three leave the office.

Brooksie is ready to go home and enjoy her pet companions. She tells her coworkers she is hoping not to find a cat named Samson happily making himself at home, but knows that her aunt has probably struck again, and Samson will be a permanent guest. She would now be the proud caretaker of six of Aunt Tilly's rescued cats.

Rachael says she is going to meet a friend for dinner and a

movie. She says, "Brooksie how would you like to double date with Richard and me sometime? He has a very nice guy friend who has a great sense of humor, just like you. He also isn't a bad tennis player. I think the two of you would really hit it off."

"Thanks Rachael for thinking of me, but I'm very busy with other commitments. Later maybe, when I have more time."

"What's with you Brooksie? You go out with us girls and have a great time, but never let any one of us fix you up with someone."

Brooksie responds, "I like my life just like it is. I don't want complications. I do appreciate your offer, but I guess I just don't trust myself to make good choices yet."

"What's it going to take for you to move on from your past?" asks Rachael.

Brooksie answers, "Not really sure how to answer you, cause I don't know myself. Courage and a great deal of wisdom would be two great starts. Please know that I truly appreciate your interest and concern."

Anita offers, "I can understand where you are coming from, Brooksie. I'm not real confident about the choices I make either. What with school, work and my brother, there isn't much time for dates. Good-by you two, I need to get to the store. Brad's coming for dinner and I have some homework to do."

CHAPTER III

"It is the unexpressed anger that is harmful."

BERNIE SIEGEL
HEALERS ON HEALING

NEXT DAY

The office is abuzz when Brooksie enters. Rachael, Lucinda, Dan, Anita, and Virginia are all standing around Melissa's desk. Melissa asks, "Has anyone heard any more about Ray Sorensen and how he died?"

They all look towards Brooksie and she responds, "Lucinda, Virginia, and I did meet with the detectives. There is still no new information. They wanted to know why Mr. Sorensen had come to the clinic. They asked us if we had had any contact with him after he finished his grief support sessions. That was pretty much a 'no.' Actually we couldn't say very much because of the confidentiality issues involved. Detective Marino said they might need to subpoena all records regarding Mr. Sorenson and again speak to the entire staff."

"Why would they need to meet with us again?" asks Lucinda.

"They didn't say why. I assume it's routine when there has been a possible homicide. That would be my guess," responds Brooksie.

Brooksie continues, "I have an appointment to meet with Ray's mother and daughter after work. I am going to call a staff meeting soon to discuss what we can say legally. We may need to confer with a lawyer, just to be on the safe side."

Everyone gets ready to leave, when Drs. Sharon Primm and Curtis Rey ask for a minute of their time. Sharon and Curtis are both psychologists and rent office space in the same building. Sharon always acts aloof and in control, so it is surprising to see her appear anxious. She keeps buttoning and unbuttoning her jacket.

Anita walks up to Sharon and asks her if she is feeling okay.

"I may be getting a touch of the flu. Several of the clients I have seen this week are sick," answers Sharon.

Curtis asks, "What happened to Ray Sorensen and why did the police show up here?"

"Ray Sorensen's death was in Monday's paper and the police are investigating the circumstances," answers Melissa.

"I don't read the paper very often. I don't want to start my day reading bad news. Then I will just be pissed or depressed the rest of the day." says Curtis.

Sharon pales noticeably. "How did he die? What did you all tell the police about him?" she asks. Her voice is barely audible.

"The paper didn't give many details, except he had drowned and they continue to look for other bodies or survivors. Sharon you know as well as anyone that we cannot share information about our clients," says Brooksie. "The detectives said an autopsy was done, but they are waiting for lab results to come in."

Sharon brushes a piece of lint off her beautifully tailored, three piece suit. In her usual uppity voice says, "Well there will be no need for me to speak to the detectives. I never had Mr. Sorensen as a client."

As everyone is leaving the room, Lucinda asks Brooksie, and Virginia, to stay behind a minute. Melissa asks if she could stay also.

Lucinda begins, "You're welcome to stay Melissa. I want to know just how much we can share with each other, since we were the facilitators in his group?"

"I see no problem with confidentiality for the four of us to share what we remember about Mr. Sorenson. We just need to keep it between us, at least for now," replies Brooksie.

"I have very little knowledge of Mr. Sorensen. My only contact with him was at my desk," says Melissa.

"Melissa I don't believe you have anything to be concerned about," offers Brooksie.

Virginia adds, "I remember how devastated he was in the first session. Closer to the end of the twelve weeks he seemed far more hopeful and was talking about dating."

Lucinda says, "After looking briefly through my notes this morning I know we were not concerned that he harbored any suicidal thoughts, in fact, he seemed to be making plans for his future. His mother was a great support for him and his daughter. He talked about spending a lot of time with Macy and that they were very close. My last notes mentioned his concern that his daughter was upset because he had met some lady."

"I have similar memories about his concern regarding his daughter and his enthusiasm about some lady. I believe we will have time to go over our notes and refresh our memories in the next few days," says Brooksie.

Driving home Brooksie thinks about her "to do" list, which is never ending, thanks to the ever growing menagerie, gifts from Aunt Tilly. *I need to get Samson, very probably my newest addition, to the vet for an eye problem. Like most cats, he assumes my only purpose for existence is to serve his needs. I also need to run the vacuum and do a bit of dusting. Maybe I'll give Rachael or Lucinda a call and see if they have any plans for this coming weekend.*

CHAPTER IV

*"Grief is the rope burns left behind when what we have
held on to most dearly is pulled out of our grasp."*

STEPHEN LEVINE

SESSION TWO

The group members trickle into the conference room. Mary
walks in with Heidi, and Harvey follows close behind, wearing
a wrinkled shirt and is unshaven. The remaining members file
into the room one by one, barely noticing one another.

Rachael, Anita, and Brooksie greet them and after all are
seated in the circle, Rachael asks how the past week went for
each one. Silence fills the room like the eerie quiet of early
morning mist.

"Who will share how they did this past week?" she asks
again. "Difficult, sad, anything unusual happen, any surprises?"

Dell speaks up, "I had a pretty rough time of it. My daughter
is suffering and I can't seem to be of much help to her. Thank God
there are others who are reaching out to her. My mother-in-law
is a saint and several friends have really stepped in with great
support and activities for her."

Anita leans towards Dell and says, "It can feel like an
overwhelming task to console your child when you are in the
very middle of your own pain. She's fortunate to have others who
can offer a good listening ear and support to her."

Dell nods his head in affirmation.

Mary sighs, "I had a real hard time. It was our thirty-sixth anniversary, a sad day for me," she says. "My children and their families live so far away. They did call and I tried to sound okay. I put on my 'happy voice.' No sense in them suffering too, but I do wish we lived closer to each other."

Justin speaks up next. "I returned to work one week after Marinda died. My patients need me and I need to be busy. My wife's illness was only diagnosed twelve months before her death. She appeared to be really sick for a just a few months before she passed away. I still can't believe she is gone.

"My daughter, Shirley, and I have never been very close. She's sixteen, the unexpected baby. I haven't spent much time with her. Her mother was very close to her. I think the hardest part of dying for Marinda was leaving her 'baby'." He pauses and looks around the group. "This past week has been especially difficult because it was Shirley's sixteenth birthday. My sister-in-law gave her a real nice party. Of course I paid for it, but I just couldn't get into a celebratory mood. After the party and when everyone had left, Shirley started sobbing and started yelling at me, 'Why couldn't it have been you? Mom loved me and I can't stand the thought that from now on it will be just you and me. We are strangers!'

"I wanted to cry, but I know I'm expected to keep it all together. My dad taught me the importance of control. If my brother or I cried, for any reason, Dad would humiliate us. Mom even told us to hide our tears. I think Mom was really afraid of Dad. She never really showed any kind of emotion." Justin's face remains expressionless as he talks. "As I said before, they traveled a great deal and my brother and I were sort of 'house-sat' by a nanny and housekeeper. They were both efficient, but kept their emotional distance, probably at my parents' request. Marinda was the opposite of my parents. She wore her heart on her sleeve and never acted embarrassed by her own tenderness. She was so easy to love. I could show my feelings to her, but I could never quite feel comfortable showing feelings to my kids.

I have never been mean and cold like my folks, but I have always been fairly distant from them."

The room grows very quiet, most appear to be staring at their shoes or some spot on the floor. Brooksie notices tears running down Harvey's cheeks and onto his shirt. He slowly gets up and goes over to Justin and puts his arms around him. Justin's face turns red, like a ripe tomato, but he doesn't push Harvey away.

Heidi intensely stars at Justin, moves to the edge of her chair, and raises her voice, "For Christ sake, your daughter desperately needs to know how torn up you are by your wife's death. She needs a human father, one with feelings and compassion, and not one who is always in control of his emotions. If I was your daughter and saw you cry, I would feel connected to you and feel I could trust you enough to let you see my feelings. She needs to know that you are hurting." Heidi grabs a tissue and blows loudly into it.

Rachael follows up with, "Justin, how do you feel about what Heidi just said? And I emphasize the word feel."

"I feel frightened. Losing control of my feelings scares the hell out of me. I am aware that we are all in pain in this room and that somehow liberates me a little, but I also know we won't all fit into the same mold. I'm going to grieve my way and not how someone tells me I should."

Dell leans toward Justin. "Justin, I have a daughter who's eleven, and I know she is hurting, but there are times I just want to feel sorry for myself and I have nothing left to give her." He takes a deep breath. "I am grateful to my friends and my fantastic mother-in-law. They focus on Cherish when I just can't. Let others reach out to your daughter. You don't have to be the only one to comfort her."

"I would like to say something," Kathy spurts the words out. "Pain and loneliness seem to be getting worse even after two months. I'm afraid to be alone, but at the same time I can't stand to be around others, especially my friends and family. They get so uncomfortable when I cry or won't eat or can't sleep. I want them to be near me, but not say a word. They don't have a clue to what I'm feeling, and I just want to scream when Janet, my best friend, says 'I know what you are feeling, and you need to keep busy.' She actually wants me to go shopping and out to lunch with her. I can barely leave our bedroom, let alone leave the house. I feel better in this room than any other place, except maybe the cemetery. I would go there every day, but many days I just can't get out of my front door. I know my mother thinks I am going crazy, and she may be right. I feel crazy."

Brooksie offers a brief summation about grieving. "Grief is crazy making. Those who have not been there cannot understand. You are the only one walking, crawling, or running in your shoes. This is a solitary journey, but you can meet up with comforting strangers and friends along the way. Reach out when you can, but don't worry about it if you can't."

Several talk about feeling punished by the deaths. Marshall, stiffly sitting and picking at his cuticles says, "I can certainly relate to the punishment theme. Being gay and having my partner killed by a drunk driver has brought the fundamentalists racing toward me with hell and damnation. I have heard about God's wrath many times. Thom's own parents and brother didn't come to the funeral. His father never acknowledged our relationship. His mother's only concern was what her friends would think if they knew one of her sons was a gay man.

"I never understood how Thom had become such a caring, thoughtful, sensitive, and down-to-earth sort of person. He had grown up with the proverbial silver spoon, but he never let the money and status direct him away from his unselfish goal to help others any way he could. He was the best person I have ever known, a much better man than I."

Mary speaks up, "Well I really don't know much about the homosexual part, but love is the greatest gift of all. Just remember all the love you two had for each other. My husband Sam and I loved each other for thirty-five years. We had far more years than you and Thom did, and for that I am so grateful. I wish you could have had more years together."

The group continues their stories, sharing feelings and events for the rest of the remaining time.

The three facilitators begin their short discussion about the group meeting after everyone has left.

"I did call Heidi last week and she seemed quite pleased to receive a call," offers Rachael. "She thanked me several times over. I asked her if she would like me to call during the week again and her answer was an enthusiastic 'yes'. So, I plan to call her once a week, probably the day after the group meets. What do you both think of my plan?"

"It could be helpful, but I would be careful of getting too personal," says Anita.

"That is the very essence of our grief work, Anita, getting personal and making our compassion and caring visible. Rachael, I think you will know if your calling Heidi is truly beneficial. If in doubt, just ask Heidi and trust that she will know what she needs," replies Brooksie.

Rachael shifts in her chair. "Has anyone heard any more about Ray Sorensen?"

Brooksie shakes her head and says, "Far as I know, how he died is still unknown."

Anita asks, "Well, do they even know who he was dating?"

"No one seems to know any more or, at least, the police are not saying anything else. I wonder if his family knows anything about his lady friend, maybe just her name?" responds Brooksie.

Conversation continues a little longer and soon the three leave the office.

Anita looks up at the thick clouds that are about to give up their bountiful supply of water. "A usual day in the Northwest," says Anita.

While Brooksie is about to get into her car, she notices that

Anita and Sharon are having a rather animated conversation near Sharon's car. The conversation looked intense, with both women flinging their arms about.

CHAPTER V

"We make sense of our world by telling each other stories."

CAROL ADRIENNE
THE PURPOSE OF YOUR LIFE

MEETING WITH MRS. SORENSEN

Brooksie hesitates before knocking on the newly painted door, and takes a few deep breaths, praying that she would be able to offer a sense of hope and ongoing purpose, especially to the young girl inside. The door opens after only one short knock. A well-groomed lady, appearing to be in her sixties, introduces herself as Mrs. Sorensen and invites Brooksie in. Macy is sitting on the well-worn leather couch with a small, black dog curled up on her lap. The area around the girl's eyes appears red and swollen.

"I know you both may not have much of an appetite, so I was hoping to entice you with some great pastries from Riley's Deli," says Brooksie with the warmest smile she can muster up.

Mrs. Sorensen gazes lovingly at her forlorn looking granddaughter, "They do look good. Macy, we haven't eaten today, so how about we share something?"

"Grandma, I just can't. Maybe later."

"Macy, I'm so terribly sorry about the death of your Dad, and my heart goes out to you," Brooksie says in a soft voice. "Mrs. Sorensen, your son is well remembered by our staff. He was in my grief support group, along with two other staff members, Virginia and Lucinda. They both send their condolences and prayers."

Macy blurts out, "Maybe they have the wrong person. Maybe the dead man had stolen Dad's boat, and Dad is trying to get back home this very minute. Maybe he is with THAT woman, the secret one. I hate her."

"Macy your father has been definitely identified, using dental records, and your grandmother is going to identify him this afternoon."

"I want to see my Dad for myself."

Mrs. Sorensen asks Brooksie if she would accompany them to view Ray.

"Yes. I will be glad to accompany you both. It is not unusual for the young to want to see their deceased parent. Sometimes it really helps to make the death final and permanent, so that healing can begin. Macy, your father had been lying in the water for a long time, so he will not look much like your dad. Did he wear a wedding ring?"

"Yes, he did."

"Then, perhaps seeing his finger with the ring on it, will be enough for you. We can go in my car, and you can decide, at the time, just what you want and need to do. Is that okay with you Mrs. Sorensen?"

Mrs. Sorensen adds, "Perhaps we both need to say goodbye to him together. Macy wasn't permitted to see her mother's body after she died, and I think that was a mistake."

Brooksie asks, "Macy, you mentioned some lady. Do you know who your dad was seeing?"

"Her name was Victoria, but Dad never brought her home, and he never took me with him when he went out with her."

"What about you Mrs. Sorensen?"

"No, I didn't meet her either. I have already told this to the detectives. Ray told me it was too soon to bring her to meet us. He said she loved to sail, was very outgoing, liked to hike, and basically liked much of what he liked to do. I know Macy felt hurt and left out. She had always gone everywhere her parents went and continued to go with her dad after Valerie died. But, after he started going out with Victoria or maybe it was Vicky, he seemed to only want to be alone with her, and ignored Macy. I don't know why he was acting that way. I thought maybe it had to with his grief and missing Valerie. I thought it strange we never met Victoria. My feeling was that she was the one who didn't want to meet us. Sounds crazy, but I know my son and such a change of behavior was very unlike him.

"Another question. Why hasn't that woman called about him? Something doesn't feel right," continues Mrs. Sorensen.

Brooksie offers hope that the detectives will soon come up with some answers.

They left for the coroner's office. Brooksie suggests they stop for dinner after the identification is made. "I know a small, quiet restaurant near where we are going."

"Do I have to eat?" Macy asks Brooksie.

"No, but I would encourage you to drink water, or maybe even a milk shake or a dish of ice cream."

"Well, a strawberry shake does sound pretty good," concedes Macy.

The trip to the Coroner's building seems to go quickly. The young girl and older grandmother hold hands, and both appear to be practically holding their breath.

It is decided that grandmother will be the first to do the viewing followed by Macy, if she so chooses. Mrs. Sorensen slowly, unsteadily, walks into the room where her son has been placed for her viewing. He is covered completely, with the exception of a small part of his face and one hand. The uncovered fingers display a ring.

Brooksie takes Mrs. Sorenson's trembling hand, and notices that hers isn't all that steady either.

"The face doesn't look like my son, but I do recognize his hand because of the ring. This ring belonged to my father and is quite unique."

Detective Marino enters the room quietly, and stands near the door. He's over six feet tall, lean, and muscular. His hair is the color of dark chocolate, same as his eyes. There is something in the way he carries himself that speaks of self-confidence. Perhaps it is the way he looks directly into the eyes of another, without being intimidating.

"My son had a scar on his right leg. He was eleven years old, skiing, and ran into a tree. May I see if that scar is there?"

The detective walks over to the body, and pulls the sheet away from the spot she mentioned. There is the scar. She begins to cry, a mother's cry for her child, it comes from deep within the womb that bore the infant.

I notice that Ray has salt and pepper colored hair, unusual for such a young man. "Mrs. Sorensen, would Macy recognize her father's hair?" She said she believes so, because Macy would often tease her father that he was getting old. We agree to cover his body completely, except for the top of his head and his ring finger. Macy was led in by Detective Marino. He guides her ever so gently near her father's graying head.

Macy, pale-faced and tearing savagely at her cuticles, allows the detective to lead her to the head of the examining table. She stares at the draped body for a moment, then, gently touches the exposed hair. Quickly she turns into her grandmother's arms. The silence is deafening for a short period, Then, suddenly broken by heart wrenching sobs.

A summary of the preliminary toxicology report is handed to Mrs. Sorensen by the detective. Macy asks to go to the restroom. A female officer accompanies her.

The summary of the Coroner's report and toxicology findings stated;

1. Overdose of Zonact, 8 to 10 gms ingested.
2. Blunt force wound to left side of head.
3. Minimal blood alcohol content.
4. Abrasions and bruising on back of heels and buttocks.
5. There was no sea water present in the lungs.

On a separate sheet of paper, a handwritten note states, "The evidence does not identify the specific cause of death; whether by suicide, accident, or homicide, drowning is ruled out. Death occurred before entering the water. Foul play can't be ruled out, at this time."

Mrs. Sorensen wipes her eyes and says, "Ray never took drugs, nor overindulged himself in alcohol. He was practically a health freak. No way would he kill himself. His daughter meant the very world to him. This was no accident. He was such a good man, great son, husband, and father. I keep thinking, or hoping, I'm going to wake up, and end this nightmare."

CHAPTER VI

*Loneliness...is and always has been the central
and inevitable experience of every man*

THOMAS WOLFE
YOU CAN'T GO HOME AGAIN

SESSION THREE

Heidi, Marshall, and Mary stroll into group at the same time, and take adjoining seats. Harvey and Justin walk from the parking lot together, and also sit next to each other. They seem lost in their conversation. The rest follow into the room. Mary has brought some homemade cookies that look inviting and smell of cinnamon. There is no doubt that certain foods are truly comforting, and homemade cookies definitely fill that bill.

Rachael waits till all are sitting down, in the chair of their choice, and then asks for volunteers to share what the past week had been like, and to also tell a little about their partner, who died. "This will help the group get to know the person you have lost. I'm letting you know in advance, that for our fifth session, you will be asked to bring a memento. Something you would be comfortable sharing with this group. I will offer a few ideas; a sweater, a picture, anything that reminds you of the one who died, and perhaps something that comforts you. We like giving you two weeks to decide what you might want to share."

Heidi begins to cry immediately. "Our wedding date is next weekend. I just want to go to bed, sleep for a week and wake up when the fifteenth has passed."

Hearing the pain in Heidi's voice turns Brooksie's dark brown eyes moist. Brooksie looks into Heidi's baby blues and tells her, "There are dates, holidays, and other special events that will bring you to your knees, and you can pray, beg, or use it as a starting position. Your choice, your grief. Heidi, the fifteenth will probably be meaningful for a long time to come. Sometimes planning ahead for a special day can actually relieve the terror or whatever else you may be anticipating. Is there anything you could plan to do on the fifteenth to help yourself and to honor the love you and Rolf shared?"

"Would you like to go to my church that day with me? We could go to lunch, or dinner, or just go to the cemetery and cry together," offers Mary. She tenderly takes hold of Heidi's hands. Heidi does not resist.

"Perhaps we could all go to the cemetery. Heidi, would that be okay with you?" Marshall asks.

"I would also feel privileged if you would let us join you," said Justin. "I'm thinking selfishly now. It would help me, too, because I haven't been able to go visit my wife's grave. My daughter has asked to go, but I keep putting her off. I dread going to the cemetery."

"I want to say yes, but I don't know if I can really go there. I'm afraid of how crazy I might act. But, I could try. I want to try."

"I would be happy to pick you up," said Dell. "Would it be okay if I bring my daughter?"

Heidi looks at Rachael. "Do you think I can do it, and should I?"

"What does your gut, your heart, say?"

"My mind says, no. 'You idiot, are you crazy?' But, deep inside I sort of like the idea of spending my wedding date with my fiancée even if I can't see him."

Heidi folds her hands in her lap, stares at them, and takes a few deep breaths. "Yes, Dell, please bring your daughter." Heidi looks over at Justin, and in a barely audible voice says, "Please bring your daughter as well, Justin. Rachael, would you also come?"

"I'm sorry. I will be out of town this coming weekend, but I will call you just before I leave."

Anita and Brooksie ask Heidi if she would mind if they tagged along.

She answers, "I am grateful for any and all support."

Kathy is picking the nail polish off of her fingernails, her eyes cast downward. She hesitantly speaks, "I'm sorry. I'm too raw, too angry, and sick at heart. I just can't get to that place yet. I can barely get through an entire day without screaming or sobbing. I'm so angry, and so frightened that I can't make it without Dick. He was perfect for me. We laughed a lot and liked doing most everything together. He was so handsome and strong. He encouraged me with whatever goals I set for myself. He helped me to do things I had never thought I could. We were both taking flying lessons and, of course, he learned much faster and was better. I was doing okay, but I was scared to death. I wanted him to be as proud of me as I was of him. We were both looking forward to starting a family.

"We were having some friends over for dinner the day he died. I had forgotten to go the liquor store and he offered, cheerfully, to go for me. I wanted to make a special rum drink and forgot to buy the rum. He didn't return. I thought maybe he had run into friends or, worse, he had been involved in some kind of accident. After he was an hour or so late I decided to go and look for him. The liquor store was about fifteen minutes away. When I got near I saw police cars everywhere. My heart started to pound, like it is right now. When I got close, I saw his car, and my heart started to pound. I couldn't catch my breath and I felt like I might throw up. A wave of something passed through me. I don't remember all the details from then on. A policeman was holding me, and I was struggling to get away from him. I told him my name and asked what happened and was anyone hurt?

He gently, but firmly moved me into a patrol car, made me sit down, and told me my husband had been shot and killed. The policeman had a neighbor of mine, who had been near the store, sit with me. The rest is a blur. I know I pleaded to just hold him and see that it was really him. I had to see him for myself. I didn't really believe that it was Dick who had been killed. Someone had to have made a mistake. No way was my Dick dead. We had too many plans for our future.

"I keep replaying things over and over. 'If this only' and 'if that only,' driving myself and others crazy. If only I had not forgotten the rum, I wouldn't be telling this story now." She sucked in a room full of air, slowly exhaled, let her head fall back, and let out a wail. The wail could have torn the heart strings right out of anyone within hearing distance.

The depth of Kathy's intense anguish touches everyone in the room. A mile high wave of invisible sadness covers the group. The tears that follow were not only for Kathy, but for everyone, in the room, at that moment.

Rachael speaks softly, "What you are saying makes good sense. Learning day by day to manage the feelings and the unanswerable questions, the 'what if's,' are a full time job. The 'what if's' do have a place. They are necessary and eventually will probably wear themselves up and fade. The 'what if's' and 'why for's' are just part of the sorting that has a place in your personal grief work. A few may not need, nor want to ask, those particular questions, and that is also okay.

"Remember grief is a process, a personal process. Figuring out what questions are important to you is up to you, and only you."

"I play the 'what if' and 'if only' games daily. Seems like it is stuck in my head," says Marshall. "I don't know how to quit these repetitive thoughts."

Anita shares that some times when she has bothersome,

frequent thoughts she simply embraces them and asks herself, "what can I learn from this?"

"I exaggerate the thoughts, and lean into the feelings and thoughts. I simply give myself over to them. Brooksie calls it a necessary pity party."

Harvey speaks of going on a day trip with son, Hank. He says they both need some time away from the house and all the memories. "I will be back in time to go to the cemetery with you, Heidi, and whoever else is going."

The session has come to an end. A few remain, making transportation plans for the trip to the cemetery. Eventually the room empties and Anita, Rachael, and Brooksie do their debriefing and observation routine.

They, of course, talk some about the death of Sorensen. "Do the police have any suspects yet? Why aren't they telling us more?" Anita asks.

Rachael replies, "I know for a fact that many murders go forever unsolved. We may never know who killed him. My heart really goes out to the daughter. How could Ray Sorensen date someone so soon after his wife's death and ignore his own daughter's feelings. I mean, that is cold."

"Sounds like her plight touches close to home, Rachael."

"Brooksie, I am just making a comment. Yes, my mom did die when I was young, and my dad was a jerk. I can simply remember how badly I felt for a long time. I'm over it now, but there is definitely some scar tissue left over from my childhood. Most of us here at the clinic have some old wounds."

Driving home after work, Brooksie thinks to herself, *many of the staff had rather difficult childhoods. I guess it makes sense that we are drawn to the profession that deals with old hurts.*

I knew Rachael's mom died when she was about ten years old, and her dad raised her. She left home at age seventeen, because she couldn't get along with the stepmother. She married young and divorced after a few years. She seldom talks about her private life, except for some guy, Richard something? She never sounds that thrilled with him, in fact, her remarks seem guarded when anyone asks her about Richard.

Then, there's Lucinda, who is more verbal about her social life. Seems she dates once in awhile, but has no special guy. Both women are active: water sports, skiing, hiking, and more. Neither have children.

Rachael is an excellent advocate for abused children and Lucinda specializes with families with children.

Dan has been a social worker for over twenty-five years. He has been married twice. Chris has been his wife for the past ten years. He has three grown children by his first wife. I vaguely remember her name is Veronica, maybe it's Victoria or something similar. He doesn't speak very kindly of her. He told me once that her jealousy ruined their marriage.

I believe his mother also died when he was a young teenager, and he has been estranged from his father for many years.

I have my own issues with deaths and loss. I have always been drawn to those people who have had their hearts broken, in one way or another. I guess many are wounded in some way or another.

As Brooksie pulls into her driveway, there sits Aunt Tilly's old Ford. *I knew she would somehow talk me into keeping old Samson.*

"Hi, Aunt Tilly. I suppose you've been visiting Samson. I must say he and his new litter mates are getting along famously."

"Hello. My dear child, you know that you fall in love with every precious creature I bring to you and Samson is no different."

Samson is much improved since her aunt had left him at Brooksie's house. He had been a rather disheveled, three-legged, timid cat. Now he hops right up to sit on her lap, without needing an invitation. She pats him tenderly and immediately a jet-engine sounding purr can be heard throughout the house. Aunt Tilly and Brooksie both know that Samson is in his permanent home.

"Would you like to stay for dinner, Aunt Tilly, and, by the way, where is Uncle Joe?"

"No thanks, dear, I don't have the time. Your uncle and I have a meeting at the local animal shelter tonight. You know we are trying to raise community funds to help with the spaying and neutering of discarded dogs and cats. The people who adopt pay a fee, but it doesn't cover the neutering expenses."

"You both do such a grand job of helping God's forgotten critters. I love you both even more because of your big hearts. Now, having said that, please don't bring anymore of the darlings to me."

"By the way, Brooksie, the vet told me Samson needs some dental work done in the near future. He is going to remove some teeth and put him on antibiotics for the gum infection. Poor Samson was malnourished before going to the shelter. They said he had probably been trying to survive on his own for a long time. Thanks for taking such good care of him, my dear. Don't forget Sunday dinner."

"I'll be there. Is there anything I can bring?"

"Why yes, since you ask, you can bring a date."

"Now Auntie, who is going to date someone who has a petting zoo?"

CEMETERY VISIT

The cemetery looks deserted. All had agreed to meet at the front entrance at 11:00 a.m. Anita and Brooksie arrive early to observe the members' first reactions walking on the cemetery grounds.

Harvey drives up first and goes over to Brooksie's car. She rolls down the driver's window and he leans in and says, "I hope this will be helpful for Heidi. I find my wife's grave comforting, and I feel close to Helen. She was in such pain, and now I believe she is at peace and watching over Hank and me."

Mary, Heidi, and Marshall arrive together, in Marshall's car.

Heidi looks about ready to fly apart at the seams, and Mary has her arms around her. Marshall is very solicitous of both ladies. He appears to be a little nervous, talking incessantly. Today's planned visit takes courage from each of the mourners.

Justin drove by himself, saying he was on call and might need to leave suddenly. He didn't have his daughter with him saying that she had to do something at school.

Anita and Brooksie had driven together, which gave Brooksie a chance to have a little time alone with her. Although Brooksie is only three years older than Anita, she apparently feels quite protective of the younger woman. Anita tells her companion during the ride this would be a very difficult experience for her.

"I've never visited my mother's grave. I just couldn't. Dad left right after mom died and never returned," she tells Brooksie.

"How old were you when she died, Anita?"

"I was sixteen and my brother was fourteen. Dad stuck around for a few months, but then left with no goodbye, no nothing. We were sent to separate foster homes for a short time. My aunt finally got all the required paper work done so that we could live with her."

"So you have been on your own these past nine years, you and your brother?"

"Well, sort of. My Aunt Jessie, Mom's sister, took us in. She is very different from Mom, intolerant and cold. My aunt is not the sort of person you can hug, ever. But, she does believe in hard work, education, and being responsible. She takes her role as caretaker, very seriously. She demanded we finish school and expected high grades, at least from me. She has never seemed to like my brother, Brad. She acts almost hostile to him, constantly putting him down.

"There has been little affection between us, but she does take an interest in me and has always been fair, at least to me. She let us live in her nice house, a house without laughter, lots of reading and discussions. She took me to plays, museums, and libraries, all her interests, not mine. But, she never did much for Brad except to provide food and lodging.

"Sometimes she still badmouths my dad. Even though I agree with her assessment of him, I wish she wouldn't say what she does. I don't think she likes men very much. She has never been married and I've never seen her go on a date or have a man friend.

"I always felt like a visitor in her house, and still do, that is whenever I visit her. Now I have my own apartment. It's not much, but it is mine, where I don't feel like an intruder, a bothersome guest."

"What do you remember of your mother?"

"She was fun-loving, hugged me a lot. I was happy when she was alive. She made Brad and me feel special, wanted, and loved. We didn't even know how sick she was until a few months before she died. No one told us anything.

"Dad was never around much. He apparently worked long hours for some company.

"Mom finally told us she had cancer, and it was widespread. She said our Aunt Jessie and Dad would take care of us. The seriousness of her illness didn't really sink in until her last week of life. She was so thin and sad looking. She told both of us to finish high school and go on to college. She warned us to be very careful of romantic relationships, and to take a long time to get to know someone before ever getting serious. We cried a lot those last days.

"Dad only went to see her a few times. He never even showed up when she was dying. I really hate him. Mom or someone should have told us sooner about her cancer. Being angry with her still bothers me, and I haven't been able to visit her grave, not even once."

"Anita, thanks for being so open and sharing so much with me," says Brooksie. We both have trust issues. Personally, I don't plan on letting myself get hurt the way I have in the past. My mom didn't really try to understand me ever. She physically took good care of me, but not emotionally. I think she did the best she could. She was more like an ostrich; when trouble came, she put her head in the sand and waited for the bad to pass over. The few men in my life have been sort of like her. They only stuck around for the good times. In times of difficulty they would stick their heads in the sand, and I would feel all alone again."

"I know what you mean. My aunt treats me okay only if I am doing what she wants me to. I'm not a fair-weather friend, and I don't think you are either," responds Anita.

"You've got that right."

"You know that Sharon, Dr. Primm, says that her sister is really hung up on her old hurts, too," says Anita. "Sharon tells her sister that old grudges only hurt the one who is keeping the grudge. I'm trying to forgive my Dad, but it's not easy," Anita blew out a long breath.

"I didn't realize you were on a first name basis with Sharon Primm."

Anita takes a minute to respond, "Sometimes we go for coffee or a meal. She is very supportive of my educational goals. In fact, if it weren't for Sharon, I might have quit school months ago. She loans me books and gives me pep talks constantly. I know some of the women at the clinic think she is stuck-up, but she has been really great to me and great for me."

More of the members continue to arrive at the cemetery. Anita and Brooksie continue to watch the solemn group as they follow Heidi to the grave site of her fiancée, Rolf. They all look like the walking wounded, heads down and shoulders slumped. Anita and Brooksie get out of their car and join them standing in front of Rolf's marker.

Mary reminds Heidi she is not alone.

Tears trickle down Heidi's cheeks and in barely a whisper she says, "Rolf, how could you leave me? I thought you loved me. I needed you and I thought I was enough for you. I'm so lost and so angry. I want to forgive you, and I want to understand. But nothing makes any sense to me. I'm so tired of being angry. You shot both of us, and that was really selfish."

Cherish and Dell cling together, weeping without restraint. Cherish places a small bouquet of flowers on Rolf's grave. She whispers into her dad's ear, "Do you believe mom can see us? Does she miss us like we miss her?"

"I don't know, honey, but I do know she loved us with all her heart and didn't want to leave us."

Justin steps a few paces back and speaks to Anita and Brooksie. "I never knew how painful grief could be. Death feels like failure to me. I am trained to help people survive, to cure, to repair, to fix. I couldn't even help my own wife, and my daughter, Shirley, must be feeling like Dell's daughter. What can I say to lessen her pain?"

"I think there are times when words get in the way. Holding each other, crying, or laughing together conveys the true feelings of understanding and caring. Why don't you just tell her you don't know what to do or say, but would like to hold her, just hold her? You both may feel awkward at first, but it will get easier with practice," answers Brooksie.

Marshall also steps away from the grave site and says to Justin, "Maybe you could both get professional help, at least for your daughter. Someone who is good with young people."

Dell adds, keeping his voice to a whisper, "Good suggestion, Marshall, not only for Justin's daughter, but also for mine. I already have a call in to Dr. Rey for Cherish. She likes the idea of talking to someone besides her grandmother and me, about her feelings."

Everyone remains quiet for a time. Slowly all eyes turn to Heidi and Brooksie.

Brooksie asks Heidi if she is ready to leave. "You need to tell us what you want to do now."

"I'm ready to go home. I am very tired and I think I will go back to bed for awhile. I'm really glad that I came, and thanks to all of you for encouraging me and for coming with me. For some reason, my head feels lighter and my headache is gone."

Heidi had brought a picture of Rolf and herself from a happier time. She places it on the grave.

As we all walk back to our cars, the heaviness in the air seems slightly lighter. Mary says she is going to spend the next few days and nights with Heidi. Heidi seems pleased and relieved to have Mary's loving company.

After driving Anita back to her place, Brooksie remembers a saying she heard some time ago. *It had to do with, "sorrow shared is halved, and joy shared is doubled." I don't remember the author. However, it really seems to hit the nail on the head, after today's cemetery visit. I also remember Rachael's comment about most of the staff have old wounds caused by the loss of a parent when they were fairly young and completely vulnerable. There are definitely strong emotions tied to this early loss.*

CHAPTER VII

"He who lacks time to mourn, lacks time to mend."

WILLIAM SHAKESPEARE

A SECOND VICTIM

Brooksie is at home, sitting on the floor, surrounded by her menagerie, contemplating her circumstances. *I don't have much of a social life, no guys are knocking down my door. At least my private life isn't very complicated. I have all I can handle comfortably with work, house, yard, and pets. I must admit that Detective Marino is very interesting. He is not hard to look at, great forearms, and riveting dark brown eyes, almost black. There is a kindness behind those intense eyes. I can't imagine what he has witnessed, but I think he has somehow retained his compassion. He is probably happily married with four children, or gay.*

I love my assortment of creatures that Aunt Tilly is so cleverly filling my home and life with. Animals are so generous with the giving and receiving of affection, even including a now-and-then wet kiss. Licks and kisses from my pets are endearing, as long as I keep myself from thinking about the last place their tongues have been. Samson has simply made himself, with no effort, a family member. I don't believe he ever considered himself an outsider, and he certainly doesn't worry about a missing leg. Animals are much more accepting of adverse conditions.

Back at work, in Brooksie's office, she and Anita are talking about their experiences at the cemetery, when Dan knocks on the door.

"Excuse me, ladies, you need to hear this. I just spoke with a lady who said she was the mother-in-law of Jim Marcus. She told me Jim died a year ago, and that he had been in a support group at this clinic. She said that she had just read about Ray Sorensen, and the news gave her chills. She stated that Jim also died several months after attending our support group. She continued on to say that her daughter died, and Jim wisely joined a widower's support group. Jim's brother never believed Jim's death was an accident, even though that is what is written on the death certificate. She would like to speak with someone at the clinic. Of course, I agreed that an appointment should be made as soon as possible. I told her that our secretary would call her back today and set up a time. Could you please ask Melissa to call her back and set up the appointment?"

He goes on to say, "I'm thinking, how could two men, who had attended one of our groups, die in 'accidents' a month or so after finishing the twelfth session? This sounds a bit strange, too much of a coincidence."

Brooksie asks Melissa to retrieve the chart of Jim Marcus and make an appointment for Mrs. Rinaldi for tomorrow in the late afternoon.

Dan says, "I'll let Lucinda and Virginia know about the appointment with Mrs. Rinaldi."

Brooksie asks Dan, "Would you mind if I join your meeting?"

"Brooksie, thanks for offering and we will be glad to have you. The more the merrier. You know I love a room full of fine women," replies Dan.

Later, Dan glances over the chart and tells Lucinda and Virginia, "Just like Mrs. Rinaldi remembered, we three were the group facilitators. Marcus was in a group about one and a half years ago. He asked for a referral for his daughter, because she was having some jealousy problems. We gave him the name of three other psychologists, including Dr. Primm. Sharon doesn't work with children, but she does do research on young boys and girls who have lost a parent. She is always gathering information for research and, eventually, her book. I'm not clear as to what the focus of her book will be."

Later that morning, Brooksie again thinks about the issues of old wounds, and the possibility of widowers being targeted. *It seems bizarre someone could have a grudge against mourners, widowers in particular. Maybe I've read too many mystery novels. I'm jumping to a conclusion without all of the facts. My Aunt Tilly would say, "Trouble will find you soon enough so don't go and send out invitations." I better inform the detectives about this right away.*

CHAPTER VIII

*Happiness is beneficial for the body, but it is grief
that develops the powers of the happy mind.*

MARCEL PROUST
*REMEMBRANCE OF THINGS PAST:
THE PAST RECAPTURED*

SESSION FOUR

GRIEF PROCESS

Rachael cheerfully announces, "Welcome all, we are starting our fourth session. I want to remind you all that everyone manages his grief feelings in a somewhat different way, though there are similarities. Some days there seems to be progress, a sense of continuing life, a brief moment of enthusiasm for something that used to be enjoyed or looked forward to. The very next hour, day, or month can feel almost worse than before. I do speak from experience. One step forward, two steps back. Eventually two steps forward and one half-step back.

"Where do you feel you are, in this so-called grief dance? How can each of you measure your individual progress? How can you know that you're truly doing the grief work necessary, so your life will once again fill with joy, anticipation, laughter, purpose, and hope?"

Heidi was first to answer, "I can definitely measure progress, if that is what you call it. I visited Rolf's grave, something I have not been able to do, even if it did take a 'team' to get me there. I can now talk about my anger at Rolf, and I see that as a big step forward. I have felt so guilty about my feelings, and now I understand that anger is natural, and, by denying it, I kept it growing. Once it was out in the open, it has begun to lessen."

Justin speaks up, "I learned a great deal on our visit to the cemetery with Heidi. I saw Dell comfort his daughter, and it hit me like a brick right in the chest, I need to hold my daughter to comfort her, for her sake, as much as for mine. Since Marinda's death, I have sorely missed human touch. I just couldn't admit it, especially since I wasn't all that touchy-feely with my children before their mother died. Marinda easily gave and received affection. That was one of the traits that I loved about her.

"After the cemetery visit, and when I was home, I did find a moment alone with Shirley and asked her if I could hug her. At first she looked stunned and shied away, and we both were embarrassed. But we talked and I kept offering my arms, and finally she let me give her a bear hug. She sort of crumbled in my arms, and we both cried our eyes out. We talked for a long time about our sorrow and fears. It was one of my best days, ever."

"No one ever gets too old for hugs," says Mary. "I miss walking hand-in-hand, snuggling in bed and putting my feet between his legs to warm up my chronic cold feet. Heidi, you showed courage and strength by going to Rolf's grave."

Brooksie adds, "Managing feelings can be like riding an out-of–control roller coaster. Flying high to the top peaks and then dropping instantly to the depths, all coming from the same ride. I would like each one of you to write one to three or more words, on the paper just handed out to you. Describe your present feelings, using conditions of nature. Close your eyes and try to focus on what you are feeling. Give that feeling a name, related to Mother Nature, and add the season it fits."

Kathy immediately blurts out, "I don't need two minutes, my

words are volcano, glacier, burning heat, and ice, two extremes. All seasons are rolled into one."

Harvey gives, "Beginning spring, buds."

Mary offers, "Drought after the flood, and my season is summer."

Heidi says, "Powerful snowstorm that is weakening, end of winter."

Marshall contributes, "Desert sandstorm, visibility poor and hard to breathe, season unknown."

Dell, replies, "Uncharted waters, cloudy, and foggy, winter."

Justin says, "Hurricane, house blown away, the season for the terrible storms."

After the members finish vocalizing their descriptive words for their feelings, an insightful discussion follows.

Brooksie shares a little about her own grief experiences. "The process of grieving never seemed to go in a straight line. One day I felt spring was arriving and the next moment winter hit me smack in the face, steps forward, steps backwards.

"Ask yourself how much time are you spending in one season? The answer will give you an idea about your personal progress. Progress does not imply forgetting. It simply means, while you are remembering, continue to live in the present, despite the absence of a loved one."

CHAPTER IX

There is no right way to grieve, but
There is a wrong way.

MEETING WITH MRS. RINALDI

Mrs. Rinaldi has brought in a newspaper clipping about Jim hiking in the Mt. Rainer Park, and apparently falling to his death. It mentioned that his wife had died a year before. The article also stated Mr. Marcus's daughter told the police that her father was supposedly going to take a lady friend to go mountain hiking with him. A possible female companion was never found.

Mrs. Rinaldi asks the therapists if she should go to the police, with her suspicions. Brooksie immediately agrees she could call the department and ask for Detective Marino or Detective Swain. Dan and Lucinda express their concerns about the clinic's reputation and their joint concerns for the present clients.

"I believe the detectives are keeping the safety of our clients in mind," answers Brooksie.

Mrs. Rinaldi says, "I'm not sure what to say to them. They may think I am just some crazy old lady. Could one of you please make the call?"

After a brief, but lively discussion, all agree that this is, indeed, a matter for the police.

Brooksie places a call to the Homicide Department. Detective Swain takes the phone call and listens to her, as she briefly relates Mrs. Rinaldi's suspicions and that of Jim's brother. Brooksie hands the phone over to Mrs. Rinaldi and offers encouragement with a gentle pat on the older lady's shoulder.

When Mrs. Rinaldi was finished she hands the phone back to Brooksie saying "He is asking to speak to you now."

"Hello again, Detective Swain."

"Would it be convenient for you to make an appointment for Mrs. Rinaldi for tomorrow, at the clinic?

If possible, it would be helpful if the staff that had been present in Mr. Marcus's group could also be present," inquires the detective.

They agree to meet early the next morning before any clients are scheduled to arrive at the offices. Mrs. Rinaldi says she is glad to be able to meet so quickly. The meeting is set for 8:00 a.m.

On her way home after work that night, Brooksie is thinking about the many terrifying possibilities that are beginning to run around in her head. *Is it possible someone is stalking our clients? What if some maniac has something against the clinic or one of the staff? I need to remind myself that I am a therapist not a policewoman. The detectives are trained to solve the crimes of violence. I'm no Columbo.*

Basically I know little about the people I work with.

Rachael is very passionate about abused kids. She had a difficult time in her teen years. Her stepmom treated her badly, she has shared a little of her anger at her dad for allowing the stepmom to be so mean to her. She doesn't seem to have much love for men in general.

Then there is Lucinda, who is really hard to get close to. I know she is divorced, and, if she dates, she keeps her private life private.

Dan lost his mother when he was fifteen and he said he is estranged from his dad.

Sharon and her sister, Maureen, lost their mother when they were very young. Sharon has briefly mentioned Maureen having a few problems. Sharon gives few details.

Even Virginia felt abandoned by her mother who developed Alzheimers.

There are many motherless staff members, all working at the clinic. I wonder how many of them have unresolved issues connected to their parental losses.

I need to get more information about the widowers in all the ongoing groups. Dell fits the description of the two murdered victims, he has a young daughter and is a recent widower.

I feel a strong need to protect the mourners who come to us for comfort and peace.

CHAPTER X

God gave us memory so that we might have roses in December

JAMES M. BARRIE,
SPEECH (1922)

SESSION FIVE
MEMORIES

The animated group fills the room, everyone carrying different sized packages, or bags. Marshall arrives with a 10 x 12 framed picture of Thom.

Anita announces, "I can see many of you brought really interesting objects to share with the group. Who would like to start?"

Heidi is carrying a 3 x 5 of her fiancée on a surfboard, and she offers to go first. "It's my favorite picture. He looks so happy. He had a boyish grin, and I brought something else to share that is very important to me."

She unfolds a beautiful lace bridal veil. The room falls silent, and then slowly the sounds of muffled crying are heard throughout the room.

Dell was the first to speak in a choked up voice, "I can only imagine how sad you must feel, holding the veil that represents your dream of a long and happy life with Rolf. I distinctly remember my wife's wedding gown and veil. She was the most beautiful person in the world. I brought our wedding picture, but now I don't feel it would be very kind to show it today, Heidi. I am so moved by your unused veil. Sorry I interrupted you. I just got so carried away with my own stuff."

Heidi smiles a sad smile. The corners of her mouth appear to turn up and down, at the same time. "That's okay, Dell, this is why we are here in this group to say what we need to. But the fact is, this veil, though it brings instant tears, also represents past dreams, present reality, and future possibilities. I was looking through veiled eyes before, and now I'm beginning to see things more clearly. I am strong enough now to face the light of day."

Harvey interjects, "I also brought our wedding picture. We grew into best friends. I loved her more the day she died than the day I married her. Here is also a picture of the three of us at Hank's graduation from high school. She was so proud of our son. He is very much like her; gentle, practical, kind, and wise beyond his years. Sometimes it is hard to look at pictures of Helen; I feel a stabbing sensation in my heart. I am looking forward to the time when I can look at pictures of our life together, and not feel so wounded. I am grateful for every day we had together."

Mary, with an inborn sweetness, says, "I brought our anniversary pictures, our first, our twentieth and, our last one, the thirty-fifth. Sam looks terrible, he refused to eat right. I cooked healthy meals, I asked him to walk with me and to quit smoking, but it was something he was always going to do 'Tomorrow.' Now there are no more tomorrows for him or for us. Our kids also nagged him many times to quit smoking, to start an exercise program, and to pay attention to what he ate. He said he appreciated their concern and never got mad at us for badgering him. He just always would put us off. I wondered down deep if he loved me as much as I loved him. If he really loved me, wouldn't he have taken better care of himself?"

Anita asks Mary, "Did you ever ask him that question directly?"

"Sort of, but actually, not really. Guess I was afraid of his answer, and it always sounded like I was laying a guilt trip on him."

Kathy raises her hand and says, "I want you to know this was a real hard assignment. I still can barely look at Dick's clothes. Even his worn out toothbrush brings me to tears. I swing from furious to practically paralyzed. I believed we were going to grow old together. We have no children because Dick wanted to wait for the right time. I never could figure out when would be the right time. I had secretly quit my birth control pills, but now I am ashamed that I was willing to deceive him. He died almost two and a half months ago. It seems like yesterday, and yet it feels like forever."

She stops talking and, almost in a whisper, says, "Please excuse me, I need to use the rest room."

"You do look pale. Do you want someone to go with you?" Rachael asks.

"No, I'll be just fine in a minute."

Brooksie decides to follow her into the bathroom anyway, just in time to hear her vomiting into the toilet.

"How long have you been nauseated Kathy?"

"No big deal. It comes and goes. Some days I don't have any problem, but afternoons seem to be when I get sick to my stomach. This has only been for about three to four weeks. I know that emotions can really affect our bodies, so I believe that pretty soon I'll feel much better."

"Do you know when you had your last period?"

"Actually, no, I think I had a short one soon after Dick died."

"Do you have a family doctor?"

"No. Dick and I had no reason to see a doctor except the doctor who prescribed the birth control pills for me. Well, I guess I could consider him a family doctor."

"I am recommending that you make an appointment soon with him. Just as a precaution, nothing to really worry about. Grief does affect the body functions, as well as the mind and spirit. I don't believe that there is anything at all the matter with you. Death of a loved one is definitely traumatic and affects our immune system. Our body, soul, and mind can become out of balance. I have known women who didn't have a period for over a year after a traumatic loss.

"Remember at our first session we suggested everyone make an appointment with their doctor for a general checkup? So that is what you need now, just a general checkup."

"Guess I forgot. I figured you were speaking to the older members. I'll make an appointment next week."

DE-BRIEFING SESSION

As usual, after the group session, Rachael, Anita, and Brooksie share observations.

Brooksie mentions her suspicion about the reason for Kathy's nausea, possible pregnancy. "We must follow up to make sure she does see her doctor. Kathy's family lives far away, so there may be only minimal support from them. In my opinion, she seems to need encouragement to build a support system for herself. How do you two think she will react and feel about the news, if she is pregnant?"

Rachael answers, "I have seen Mary talk with her after sessions. Mary is the kind of person who will adopt anyone who lacks needed support. She doesn't wait to be asked. She just makes a simple offer of support without being pushy. Harvey and Marshall are both very kind and considerate and take special interest in her. Actually the three of them are like mother hens."

Anita says, "I find myself wanting to just hug her, too. She looks so lost and vulnerable."

"So what keeps you from hugging her, Anita? Rachael asks.

"I don't want to seem unprofessional."

"Haven't you seen Brooksie and me embracing the members at times?" again Rachael.

"Yes, and that makes me uncomfortable."

Brooksie suggests to Anita to find her own style of connecting to the mourners. "Try different approaches, and always remember to be sensitive first to their needs and fit yours with theirs. You don't have to be a hugger to show your compassion or to let someone know you recognize their pain and sorrow."

"Changing the subject," says Brooksie, "The deaths of our two ex-clients weigh heavily on me. I am ready for some diversions. I know the weekend is days away, but what are the two of you going to do this coming weekend?"

Rachael has a date to go to the beach. She says, "Nothing serious, just some fun and free food."

"My brother and I haven't made any plans yet. We may just hang out around home or take in a movie," responds Anita. "What about you, Brooksie?"

"Well, I have my once-a-month dinner and dance date with my fantastic neighbors. My 'date' with David and Rolland is Saturday night. They are the perfect neighbors. They have been partners for many years, and both are wonderful human beings. We three go to dinner to the same club every month, because they have one terrific band. All three of us love to dance, and since they are not comfortable dancing with each other in public, I get to take turns with both of them. I make out like a bandit, free dinner, great dancing partners, and no worries about any romantic entanglements. Those two are just about my best friends and the greatest neighbors anyone could ever ask for."

"Maybe they have some other buddies I could become friends with. God knows I could use some genuine friendships with guys. Richard has left me feeling so vulnerable. He is definitely filled with rage and that makes him scary. I have made some terrible choices in my life. Makes me wonder if I'm ever going to hook up with a decent man," says Rachael.

CHAPTER XI

"I am not perfect, but I am enough."

RACHAEL NAOMI REMEN

HEALERS ON HEALING
FOLLOWING MORNING

Mrs. Rinaldi walks hesitantly into the clinic. A sort of half smile slowly emerges on her face. She says, "Thanks to you all for taking my concern seriously and not making me feel like a fool. I feel weird or maybe a little crazy for saying anything, but it has struck me as maybe more than a coincidence. My son-in-law and Mr. Sorenson both attended a grief support group here, and both died mysteriously. Maybe I have been watching too many police shows on TV."

Dan, always the gentleman, encourages her to continue, "Please go on. What exactly happened to Jim, and when did he die?"

"He died September fifteenth, a little over a year ago, while hiking on Mt. Rainier with a lady friend. At least I think it was with someone. He told his daughter and me that he had a date with a Vicky or Lindy, and they were going to go mountain climbing over the weekend. Racine, his daughter, asked if she could go, and he said not this time, but promised that soon she would meet his friend. When he did not return Sunday night, I got worried and called the police. They told me I would have to wait another twenty-four hours before they could make out a missing person report. The officer said that, hopefully, we would get word from Mr. Marcus soon. Next day, no call, nothing. He never missed work, and I knew something bad had happened when he didn't show up for work. I filled out a missing person's report, and that afternoon they found his car at Wet Lands Park. A search was begun, but he was not found. Three weeks later, some hikers found his body at the bottom of a ravine. He had apparently fallen from a cliff high up the mountain. No woman was found, and no woman ever called the house. Racine was so completely devastated. She had lost her mother to illness and her dad to some kind of accident, all within 18 months."

Lucinda asks, "So you are not sure about the lady's name? Was it Vicky or Lindy? You have no idea who she was?"

"I did hear him speak to someone, on the phone, that he called Vicky or Victoria or maybe it was Lindy. I just can't recall for sure. I did ask him if he liked this person. He said, 'Very much so. I still love your daughter, but I miss female companionship. This woman likes to do everything I like to do.' I did tell him his daughter was feeling left out. He said that, in time, when his friend felt more comfortable, we would all go out together, and we would meet her."

Brooksie asks, "Did you ever think that your son-in-law was suicidal?"

"Absolutely not! He was in fine health. Yes, he was still grieving for his wife, my wonderful daughter, but he was beginning to move on. He was a great dad, that is, until he met this woman. It seems so strange that she never called after his death. Maybe she also died on the mountain and has never been found."

"Was an autopsy done after they found his body?" asked Dan.

"Yes, but the report said that death was caused by trauma to the head. He had several broken bones from the fall, including a skull fracture. The police never really said much. They did ask if he might have killed himself. I told them what I told you. Jim's brother, Charlie, has never quit believing that there was foul play involved. He even hired a private detective last year, but not much came of it. He wasn't able to find any woman named Vicky or Victoria that had been seeing Jim. It was like she simply vanished."

"Maybe someone, like the police, should talk with the private detective," comments Lucinda.

"I can get his name and phone number for you later today."

The two Detectives, Marino and Swain arrive at the office and apologize for being late. They had had an emergency. Introductions are made, and Brooksie sums up the questions and answers, bringing them up to speed.

Detective Swain was the first to speak, "We will be most interested in what the private investigator found. Also, we would like to speak to Mr. Marcus's brother. Do you know of anyone who has spoken unfavorably about your son-in-law? Anyone at all who might have a grudge, Mrs. Rinaldi?"

"No, I know of no one that had bad feelings towards Jim. I will have Charlie call you today as soon as I can reach him."

"Thanks. By the way, who were the facilitators of his group? We will need a list of the other members of the group, same as we have for Sorensen's group."

Dan speaks up, "It was Lucinda, Virginia and, me. Virginia is out of town, but we can ask her to call you when she returns."

"That would be just fine," responds Detective Swain.

Mrs. Rinaldi continues, "Racine is now thirteen and is having a rough time of it. Thank God, her uncle Charlie is trying to take over the father's role, and his wife is a real sweetheart. Racine is living with them. Gratefully, they always include me in all the family get-togethers and keep me in the loop with my granddaughter."

Dan is holding Jim's chart and his own notes. "I understand that all information we have on Jim will need a release from the courts, that we are not at liberty to share our written material with anyone without a court order."

Brooksie speaks up, "I did make some calls yesterday and eventually spoke to a Fred Cane. He is a lawyer whose specialty is representing medical personnel, and counseling professionals. I made an appointment with him for next week, for all who want to go. In the meantime, he stated that expectations of confidentiality are different for groups than for individual counseling. We are not acting as counselors/therapists, but as facilitators in support groups. So, in other words, we do have some leeway. He did suggest, to be on the safe side for now, to release all written material on a certain client if the court so orders with a subpoena. He added that it would be permissible to give our opinions regarding a client, just refrain from repeating anything personal the client may have talked about in group."

Lucinda says, "Then I can say, in my opinion, he did not sound like he was considering suicide. He seemed to be a devoted father and was working through his grief. That's all I feel comfortable saying. My notes have a little more."

Brooksie asks the detectives if they are thinking there is a connection between the deaths of Jim and Ray? "Are you thinking that they were both not accidents?"

Detective Marino, looking directly at Brooksie says, "Ms. Everett, our investigation is just in the beginning stages. It is much too soon to make any kind of a statement. The cooperation of all of you will be appreciated. I will add that I never discount gut feelings or coincidences." Turning his eyes on Mrs. Rinaldi, he continues, "I would like to set up a meeting with you again, Mrs. Rinaldi, your family, and hopefully the private detective the brother had hired. Then, we must again ask to meet with the staff here. A court order will arrive, in the near future, asking for all charts and any facilitator's notes that apply to both deceased clients. I am sorry about inconveniencing any of you."

Brooksie looks at Marino and says, "When you say all the staff, do you mean all four social workers, the two volunteers, and the secretary?" Thinking to herself, *I feel like a skinny legged teenager just talking to him.* "Yes." Marino answers, "And the psychologists and the cleaning staff. We need to set it up soon as possible, say tomorrow at 9 a.m.? It could take a few hours."

Dan speaks up, "Tomorrow is good for me. The early morning is the slowest for some of us so nine will be fine with me."

A short discussion follows. Brooksie says she will have Melissa notify the rest of the staff their presence is requested for the early meeting tomorrow.

"We will meet here tomorrow at 9 a.m. Also we are letting you know in advance, the meeting will be taped," says Marino.

The meeting is over, and Detective Marino tells Dan and Brooksie, "It always amazes me that people will say they don't remember anything, but, as they continue to tell their story, often many forgotten details come forward."

After everyone leaves the room, Dan displays a Cheshire cat smile that practically extends from ear to ear, "I think the detective has an eye for you."

"Don't be playing Cupid with me, Dan. The detective hardly ever looks at me. There are many great-looking females working here, far more attractive and available than me. I truly doubt he has been eyeing me, as you put it. He has an interesting face, and is not hard to look at, either. But, romance is not on my dance card now, maybe someday. Anyway he is probably married with a dozen kids." Brooksie doesn't blush often or easily, but her cheeks are aglow like Christmas lights.

Next day meeting with the detectives.

Everyone gathers per the detectives' request. Rachael is the only one not present. She has called in sick that morning.

Brooksie passes out name tags for everyone. Figuring it would help the detectives.

Detective Marino begins, "Thank you all for your time and patience with this investigation. We need to record this interview, and we ask you to state your full name every time you begin speaking. Are there any objections?"

Everyone remains quiet.

"So I will take the silence as a no vote. No to objections? Yes to keep interviewing?"

"My name is Lucinda Chavez. Has it been decided that both men were murdered or did they die accidentally, as was first thought?"

Detective Swain responds, "We will answer questions later, if we can."

"Dr. Curtis Rey is my name. We are concerned about confidentiality. We all have confidentially issues regarding our clients."

Detective Swain answers, "Why don't we just get started and see if you feel there is a problem. We can address it then, if something comes up."

"Dr. Sharon Primm is my name. What makes the police consider homicide, rather than accidents or suicide?"

"That is a good question, Dr. Primm," answers Detective Marino, "and I can't give you many details, except to say both deaths are suspicious. Family members of both men adamantly deny any possibility of suicide. I'm aware that often is the case with grieving relatives, but in these deaths there are similar circumstances that need to be investigated. Both men had begun to date some woman unseen by the families. This person never surfaced after the deaths. We would definitely like to ask said woman or women a few questions. Again, I will say that this is just a preliminary investigation because of the similar circumstances of the two deceased. Why don't we start with you, Dr. Primm, what contact did you have with either man?"

"Actually none, they were never my clients. My practice is focused on adults, mainly women with a variety of issues. I do believe that Dr. Rey did have some contact with their daughters. Since his practice is devoted to children up to age nineteen."

"Dr. Curtis Rey is my name again. Do I have to give it every time?"

"Yes," answers the detective.

Dr. Rey continues, "Yes, I did see both fathers about their young daughters. I saw Mr. Marcus for one consultation and then had three appointments with his daughter, Racine. She was having some problems in school after her mother's death. I can't divulge any more about our sessions. I also met with Mr. Sorenson for the same kind of problem. His daughter was also struggling with grief issues about her mother. Again, I can't give any more specifics about what was discussed in their sessions. I had five sessions with Macy Sorensen."

"Since you saw both men for a consultation concerning their daughters, could you give your impression of the fathers' emotional states?"

"Dr. Curtis Rey is my name again. If I had had any concerns about the men, I would have made a note of that. I made no such note. They both seemed genuinely concerned about their daughter's well-being,"

Dr. Rey finishes and Virginia is the next one up.

"My name is Virginia Braum. I was in the group with Jim Marcus. I can't add much, except he often spoke of the outdoor activities he enjoyed with his wife and daughter, and how close he was to his daughter after his wife died. He did seem to have a roving eye for some of the staff ladies. But, I didn't notice that until about the eleventh or twelfth session. To me that was a good sign he was ready to join the land of the living. He was adjusting to his wife's death. If I am remembering correctly, he did mention he had a date with someone, and his daughter didn't like the idea very much. Anita, you were also in that group because it was a larger group than usual."

"My name is Anita Pace. Yes, I guess I was, but I don't remember much. I had to miss the last four sessions for personal reasons. I do remember Racine, maybe from when she was seeing Dr. Rey. One day we had a short visit, in the parking lot. She said that she was very hurt by her father taking up with some woman and practically ignoring her. She told me he had been a fantastic father, including her in all of his free time, until he started seeing someone."

"Lucinda Chavez again. He was quite a flirt towards the end of his sessions. He asked me to go for coffee at the end of the twelfth session, which of course I declined. It would be unethical to date clients and for several reasons. The main one being mourners are very vulnerable because of their loss. That is why we repeatedly advise them to wait at least one year before making any major decisions. A romantic involvement is a major decision. Anita and Virginia seem to know far more than I do. I do know that if he had been suicidal we would have made a note of that in our records and there is no mention of any suicidal concerns."

"Dan Potter here. Marcus was quite an athlete and enjoyed a variety of sports. The whole family mountain climbed, canoed, walked, and rode bikes. They took many family camping trips, and photography was a hobby they all seemed involved in. In fact, that is how his wife was killed, taking a picture and not looking where she was going when she backed up. She tripped and went over the cliff in front of her daughter and husband."

"Melissa Shore is my name. I am the secretary. I do remember both Mr. Marcus and Mr. Sorensen. They were nice-looking, polite, and very cooperative. Mr. Marcus brought doughnuts on several occasions for all of the staff. Mr. Sorenson was very friendly and considerate. He always asked me how my day was going. That is all I can add."

"My name is Charles Marcus, Jim Marcus's brother. I never for a moment believed that my brother killed himself. He was an optimistic person, loved life, and loved his daughter passionately, as he had his wife. Yes, he was very distraught at her death, but as time went by he began to come alive again. The police seemed eager to close the books on his so-called accident. He was in great shape, a seasoned climber and cautious. He always climbed with a partner. He avoided climbing in bad weather and was meticulous about keeping his climbing gear in perfect working order. His death has never felt accidental to me."

Detective Marino asks him about a woman that his brother might have been dating.

"He did ask me if I thought it was too soon to start dating. I said that I would be glad if he did. He barely mentioned meeting someone in a bookstore or maybe he said a coffee shop. I'm not exactly sure where he first met her. He said they had hit it off right away. She liked doing lots of things he also liked to do. He also said she was a real beauty, his exact words. That is all I know about her."

Next, Marino focuses on private detective Al Smarte. "I understand that Charles Marcus hired you to look into the death of this brother, is that correct?"

"Yes, it is. Oh sorry, I forgot to say my name, Al Smarte. I didn't find out enough to come to any real conclusions. There were two restaurants where apparently Mr. Marcus took a date. Two of the employees of both places said he had been there with a woman. She was described as tall, fantastic figure, one place said she was a blonde and the other place said her head was mostly covered with a fancy kind of hat. So they couldn't be sure of the color of her hair. All agreed she was striking in appearance; high cheekbones and flawless skin. Three of the observers were men and one a woman. Even the woman said how attractive she was. I also spoke with a park ranger who remembered Marcus' car, and the 'accident'. The ranger stated a week long search was made for a possible companion or companions. He said they didn't have a sign-in-sheet posted for visitors, that week. So they had no way of knowing if Mr. Marcus was hiking alone or with others. Wish I had more information for you."

"Thank you, Mr. Smarte. As you know, every lead can help."

Sue and Brad, who clean the offices, both deny any knowledge of the two deceased men.

"Brooksie Everett is my name. I have no first-hand knowledge of Mr. Marcus. I did see him several times at the clinic, but I never had reason to converse with him. I was a facilitator in Mr. Sorenson's group and have already given my opinion on him."

Detective Swain thanks everyone for their time and cooperation. "If you think of anything else, please call us. We have left our cards with several phone numbers on Melissa's desk."

As soon as the detectives return to their car Detective Swain says, "We need the toxicology report, and we need it now, before we go off half-cocked. Sorensen could have just had a bad day. Perhaps he was drunk, fell, tried to get up but couldn't, scooted on his butt and heels, lost his balance and fell overboard. I'm also thinking about Mr. Marcus. Let's see what his autopsy has to say. It would be extremely helpful if there is a toxicology report included. Wishful thinking I'm afraid."

"Yeah. You're right, says Marino. "The toxicology results can help to fill in a few pieces of this puzzle. The family and staff paint a picture of a well-adjusted, responsible father. No one had seen him as suicidal, not even a man who drank to excess. He apparently led a healthy life style. Not the sort of guy to get shit-faced drunk while sailing alone or with a companion. How about you go talk to his co-workers, and I'll make the neighborhood rounds?"

"I'm on it, Marino. Drop me off at the office and I'll pick up a car. By the way, are you ever going to ask any of those honeys out? If I wasn't married I'd be making some phone calls. Sharon and Lucinda are the first two I would call. What about you?"

"No doubt about it, they are all definitely great-looking therapists. You and I, we have different taste. Down the road I may make a call to one of therapists, maybe. I'm not saying which one, don't ask."

CHAPTER XII

Unfortunately, hiding our feelings is somewhat like trying to keep inflated beach balls submerged in a pool – it requires a great energy and vigilance.

AUTHOR UNKNOWN.

SESSION SIX

FEELINGS CAN BE MESSAGES, INFORMATION GIVING.

Rachael asks Brooksie, "What happened at the meeting with the detectives?"

"Not that much. Everyone was asked what they remembered mostly about Jim Marcus and less about Ray Sorensen. No one seemed to feel either man was suicidal. The police still want to speak to you to get your recollection."

"But I don't really have much to tell them."

"Well, I guess they have to speak to everyone who works in the clinic. I wouldn't worry about it."

The members of the support group enter the room, talking quietly among themselves and choosing a seat.

Heidi begins, almost before sitting down, "I've had a pretty good week. I'm actually sleeping six hours a night most nights. Sure makes a difference how I feel during the day. However, I did have a real bad day yesterday. Everything made me cry. I was involved in a fender bender which was my fault. I locked my car keys in my car and had to call a locksmith. What an added expense that was. I have never done that before. Felt like I was losing it for a while."

"Yesterday was February the twelfth. Was that a meaningful date for you?" Brooksie asks.

"No, not really. Well, except that is the date my dad killed himself. Sort of ruined Valentine's Day for me forever."

"It is amazing how we think we have forgotten some events, but our memory cells kick in," says Rachael. "Some dates are burned into our memory bank. I even have a few of my own. Our subconscious is always in tune with old hurts. This is true for professionals in our field as well. Perhaps, Heidi, somewhere down deep in your heart and mind you did remember that yesterday was another anniversary of your father's suicide. This is why it is often a good idea to plan ahead for special dates. Some people find that the anticipation is worse than the actual date."

"Rachael, you are right on. I have been thinking quite a bit about my dad this past week. Having both my dad and Rolf commit suicide makes me wonder, am I cursed or am I a curse? Is there something about me that depresses others? I also was thinking, and I am ashamed to say this, but what cowards they both were. They gave up trying, and left me to deal with the 'why's' and 'what if's.' I am trying to get past my anger, but it does sneak up on me when I least expect it. The little bit of faith I have quickly disappears when bad things go down. Guess I don't have much of a belief system going for me."

Harvey adds, "When Helen was real sick and had a great deal of pain, I, too, could feel my faith in God slipping away. I was furious with God for putting my wonderful wife through such hell. I would go outside, out of Helen's earshot, and swear, bargain, plead, and beg for God to help her. It was Helen who opened my heart and eyes again. She said, 'Dying is non-negotiable. It is something we all do. The only aspect of the process that we have any control over is the attitude we choose. We are being asked to say our good-by's, long before we want to. I'm going first and one day you will follow.'"

Marshall took a long, deep breath and offers, "It seems that each of us have a few similar issues, and a few different issues that we are faced with. Heidi and I have to deal with forgiveness. I, too, have been questioning my beliefs. How could a God let my Thom be taken away by the very kind of person he had been helping? Sometimes I feel so angry at the drunk driver I want to hit somebody, anybody. I want to choke the life out of that drunk. He had three previous DUI's and still was driving around. He had no insurance. He simply drove anytime, anywhere, and probably many times drunk. Where is the justice? How come somebody so worthless is alive and Thom is dead?"

The room is silent for a few minutes, then, Kathy speaks up, "I am really beginning to feel this small group understands what I'm going through better than my family or friends. Even though our mates died in different ways, I still feel close to each of you when you share some feeling that I have, too. When I'm in this room I don't feel so alone or isolated. Dick died in such a random way and so did Thom. Where is the justice and accountability for Dick and Thom? If Dick had arrived ten minutes earlier or ten minutes later at the liquor store, the outcome would probably be different. Same for your partner, Marshall. So I have been constantly saying to myself, what if only this or that even though I know this repetition is a futile exercise."

"I have heard this many times," says Brooksie. "The 'what if's' and thinking it over and over can become a bad habit, like getting a car stuck in the mud and spinning the wheels. You are going nowhere, probably getting in deeper, and eventually wearing the car and yourself down, and still remaining stuck. I have done it myself and I imagine that Rachael and Anita have, also."

"Guilt is another habit that can take on its own life and sabotage grief work. Guilt is only valuable as long as it helps someone to stop harmful behaviors, but guilt used as a sledge hammer to beat oneself up, or someone else up, is a waste. Personally, I feel that forgiveness is a choice, a decision, each person must decide for himself or herself if forgiveness is possible or necessary," offers Rachael.

Dell joins in, "Well the shock of Marcie's death has definitely worn off for me. I am so lonely, especially at night. After my daughter goes to bed, I feel such a gnawing emptiness. I love my daughter and we do so much together, but it is not the same kind of companionship. We don't talk about growing old together, and our memories are of different events, places, and time. She even tries to fill the gap for me, but I don't want her to. She is still my little girl and needs only to think about girl things. I try to get her to invite a friend to go on our weekend trips but she says, 'no, I just want it to be you and me, Daddy.' I have made an appointment with a therapist in two weeks. We are going together, including my mother-in-law. Dr. Primm and Dr. Rey both recommended Dr. Rossi and his office is close to my house."

"Anger at my husband also creeps into me at night when I go to bed, alone," offers Mary. "My thoughts race willy nilly in every direction. During the day when I'm working, I hardly think about myself, so I feel better going to work and keeping my mind occupied. Another trying time for me is when I go to the grocery store; buying meat and stuff for one really depresses me. I feel like people are watching me and probably feeling sorry for me. I hate pity. It is like there is a big sign hanging on the front and back of me saying, 'Widow, not worth sticking around for.' Then I get mad at myself for feeling so sorry for myself. I do just fine when helping others, but it's not so easy to help myself."

Group meeting ends and both Heidi and Kathy put their arms around Mary.

Heidi says to Mary, "I have an idea, how about we three go to the market together, buy three of everything, go to my house and have dinner together.

Kathy nods her yes and Mary says, "Fantastic idea. I'll even bake us my secret, special pie."

De-briefing session

Rachael begins. "This group is beginning to bond, like Gorilla glue. They are truly supporting each other. This is the best kind of group, they do ninety percent of the talking. We can be the listeners and cheerleaders. This is so very satisfying to me. You know, Dell's situation reminds me of Ray Sorensen's circumstances. Ray was also a young man with a young daughter. He was a good dad and spent time with her doing stuff with and for her. He was the outdoors type."

"Yes," says Brooksie. "Actually, Jim, Ray, and Dell share similar situations and outdoor interests. The most obvious similarity is widowhood and having young daughters. Why would someone want to end the life of a young man who had been recently widowed and had a young daughter? It doesn't make any kind of sense. What could possibly be the motive?"

"I was in Jim Marcus's group," says Anita. "I reread our notes from the group he attended, and according to the notes, he did make emotional progress. He was dating toward the end of the last few sessions.

"Jim's mother-in-law told us he had fallen off a cliff. She thought he was hiking with a woman, but didn't know that for sure. If there were two people who had fallen to their deaths, you'd think two bodies would have eventually been found. They would have been in close proximity to each other. If that were true, then you would assume that someone would be asking about her. It's hard to believe that no one had reported her missing."

Brooksie says, "Rachael on another front, what is happening to your relationship with Richard? I haven't heard you mention him for months. If I'm remembering correctly, he was causing you some grief."

"You're right. He was causing some real problems for me. We

did have a great thing going for about a year, then, he became extremely possessive. He would start out by simply asking how my day went, but soon his inquiries turned into interrogations. What ended it for me was his temper and accusations. He was acting crazy and accusing me of sleeping around. He was particularly suspicious of any client I might be working with. Guess he finally got my message and is pretty much leaving me alone. He does call every few weeks and shoots the breeze. Last time he called he told me he was going to a therapist, and was feeling better. I'm taking a break from any serious relationships for awhile. I don't seem to make great decisions, must be bad genes."

"Sorry about your difficulties with Richard, but I'm glad he is mostly out of your life and getting some help for himself," responds Brooksie.

Anita adds, "I didn't know you were having such awful problems with some guy. Sounds pretty scary to me, how possessive he had become. Hopefully he is working through his issues."

Rachael and Anita leave Brooksie's office.

Brooksie sits alone with her thoughts for the next half hour. *I like my alone time, but it might be a nice change to go on a date with someone fun, once in awhile. Meanwhile, I need to finish planning for the neighborhood party. I've got to vacuum everywhere. My house sometimes looks like a fur factory. I'm so grateful that David and Rolland are pitching in, actually more like taking over most of the work. I'll ask my aunt and uncle to come. They are my only family, and, if I'm lucky, Aunt Tilly will find new homes for her beloved critters. My zoo is full and the no vacancy sign is out.*

She takes one last look for messages before leaving the office. One message is from Detective Swain and the other from Charlie Marcus, asking her to call back.

She dials the police department and asks for Swain or Marino.

"Detective Swain here."

"I'm returning your call. This is Brooksie Everett."

"Thanks for calling back. The toxicology report came back on Ray Sorenson. We have a few more questions. Could we get together with Virginia, Rachael, you and Curtis?"

"Yes, of course. Will Monday at noon be soon enough? I'll need to have time to verify the availability of that day and time with the others."

"Thanks. If I don't hear different from you, Monday at noon is fine."

Next, she dials Charlie Marcus. He answers on the second ring. "Hello Charles, This is Brooksie Everett returning your call."

"Thanks for getting back to me so soon. I had a visit from the police about my brother. They asked if I thought there would be a possibility of exhuming my brother's body. I'm grateful Jim's death is being reexamined, but I'm concerned about Racine's reaction to having her father's body dug up. My question for you is, what do I tell Racine about what the police are doing? My niece is thirteen and finally getting adjusted to losing both parents so close together in time. She lives with me and my wife, and life has slowly been getting back to a more normal routine. As I said before, I am glad they are finally looking into Jim's death, but I want to do the right thing by Racine. Any suggestions would be most appreciated."

"I don't know what the police are working on. The detectives are meeting with me and several staff members this coming Monday at noon. Perhaps you would like to come as well. They are not coming to discuss your brother, but you may be able to help in some way. As far as Racine goes, truth told in a gentle way is always best. If she has questions, answer them honestly and let her know she can ask you and your wife anything."

"I'll be there. I brought my niece to see Dr. Rey for a few visits, after she started living with me. Actually, Jim had initially taken her to see Dr. Rey for one or two visits while he was in the grief group. I felt she could benefit by seeing him again. See you on Monday."

CHAPTER XIII

*"To start to become aware of the ways in which our responses
to loss have shaped us can be the beginning of wisdom."*

JUDITH VIORST
NECESSARY LOSSES

Monday meeting

"This is the second time Mr. Marcus has been to the office regarding his brother's death. I hope it is okay, but I took the liberty of asking him to come to this meeting," says Brooksie.

Detective Marino graciously says, "I'm glad you're here, Mr. Marcus. We also have questions and would greatly appreciate your input along with the others. As I told you on the phone, some evidence has shown up, which is making it necessary to follow up on your brother's cause of death. Another young man has died under suspicious circumstances and there seems to be some similarities between your brother and this other person, Mr. Sorenson."

Detective Marino went on, "At first glance, the death of Ray Sorenson was ruled accidental, but new information has been ferreted out. The department is taking an in-depth look at the cause of death. I cannot share any more with you, at this time. I believe everyone present understands our purpose today is to gather not distribute information. Curtis, it's my understanding you saw Macy for a short period of time. Her grandmother said that Ray was concerned, because Macy had seemed quite disturbed and had acted out in various ways because he was dating someone. She wasn't sleeping well, her grades at school were down, and she became easily irritated. All of these behaviors were unusual for her. Do you know if Macy was taking any kind of medication?"

"Not to my knowledge," answers Curtis.

Detective Swain asks, "How did the therapy go for Macy?"

"She is a bright young girl who was, and probably still is, naturally mourning because not long after her mother died she lost her father. I will gladly surrender my file on her, as soon as I receive the request. Till then, my hands are tied, or should I say my lips are sealed?"

Detective Swain says, "Because of certain reports we are going ahead and investigating the cause of death of Mr. Sorenson. As a matter of course, we need to rule out suicide, but it seems far more plausible that we are looking at a homicide. The toxicology reports can be very valuable at ruling in or out, if drugs or alcohol could have been involved. The report is just part of the necessary puzzle that must be put together."

"Well, I can say without a doubt that my brother did not kill himself," responds Charlie Marcus, with angry overtones. "I don't know anything about Mr. Sorensen. I do know my brother would never take his own life. Since he has been dead and buried for a little over a year, can you still tell if he had drugs in his system?"

"Yes." Answers Marino. "That is a question for the lab technicians to answer in detail. We can have you speak with one before you give us the go ahead to exhume his body. Would that help you with your decision?"

"I guess so, this is really a gigantic decision for me. This is going to bring up a lot of pain for Racine and for me also. But, I will do anything to help you find the truth. You just tell me what I can do. If it is alright, I don't want to tell Racine about any of this unless some suspicious evidence turns up."

"That's a good plan, Mr. Marcus. Racine won't hear anything

from us without your permission. Lucinda or Virginia, do you remember anything more, anything at all about Mr. Sorenson?"

"Not really," answers Lucinda. "He didn't strike me as severely depressed and his neglect of his daughter seemed out of character. He spoke often about his daughter during the first ten weeks of group. He seemed very devoted to her. In fact, I did discuss his redirect of devoted attention from his daughter to an unknown lady friend with Sharon and Curtis. This change took place in the last one or two weeks of his support group. I wasn't concerned about his new zest for life; in fact, I was very happy to see him moving on with his life."

Virginia adds, "Yes, I remember that we talked about his rather abrupt change of focus around the tenth or twelfth session. Lucinda was going to refer him and his daughter to a psychologist because Mr. Sorenson said he was concerned about his daughter's behavior, since he had started dating."

Brooksie says, "It is our policy to always give the client two or three names when we make a referral. Sharon is one of the names we give to adults for therapy and Curtis is one of the psychologists who we refer families and children to."

Detective Marino says, "Let me summarize the few facts that we have up to this point. Ray and Jim, both in their early thirties, both had young daughters, and both attended grief support groups at this location. Both men were widowers, both died doing outdoor activities, both started dating an unknown woman in the last few weeks of their support group sessions, and continued to date this unknown lady up until their deaths. Neither daughter ever saw this woman. Both men died while supposedly on a date with said person. Her first name may be Victoria, Vicky, Lindy or not. No suicide notes were found, and both seemed to be dealing well with the grief and loss of their deceased wives. Lastly, both wanted a referral to a therapist for their daughters. So far we have no witnesses to their last day and zero information about any woman they may have been seeing."

Marino looks around the room at each face. "Now can anyone add anything?"

Sharon, who has been noticeably quiet up to this point asks, "Are you suggesting that someone is targeting clients from the grief support sessions?"

Marino answers, "No, I'm not suggesting anything. Investigating can be a slow process, much time is spent on interviews, fact gathering, so forth and so on, until we have enough to go to the judge with. This is strictly the beginning stage of gathering information for an investigation of the suspicious death of Mr. Sorensen. We will continue with the next logical steps, which include talking to many more people who may have had a relationship with Mr. Sorensen, and now we will also be looking into Mr. Marcus's life, as well.

"Thank you all for your time and input. Please call us if you think of anything, no matter how insignificant you think it may be. We appreciate all leads."

Brooksie sneaks a peak a Marino. She notices the outline of a gun under his jacket. Thinking to herself, *I wonder if he wears it when he goes on a date. If he dates? I'm pathetic.*

The group eventually disperses with the exception of Brooksie, Lucinda, and Anita. Both Anita and Lucinda ask Brooksie if she needs any help with organizing her house party. She thanks them and says all is under control.

CHAPTER XIV

Change is inevitable; growth is optional

CARLSON & SHIELD
HEALERS ON HEALING

SESSION SEVEN
ROLE CHANGES

Mary arrives first, carrying two delicious looking pies, fruit pies that she had made that morning.

"Baking pies and other things is one of the ways I console myself. It really helps me when sadness, frustration, or anguish overwhelms me. The wonderful smell of something cooking makes me feel at peace, like I have a purpose and can be useful."

"Feeling needed and useful is necessary for all of us," shares Rachael. "Your roles are changing and this requires patience, determination, and energy. You will need courage and an enormous amount of willingness to laugh at yourselves and at your efforts. Never be ashamed to pat yourself on the back just for hanging in there. Personally, I knit up a storm when I am upset or feel lost. The results of my knitting are practically grotesque, but my flying needles have helped me to find a more peaceful moment."

"Dell, what jobs are you doing or learning to do, that you never did while your wife was alive?" asks Rachael.

"I never cleaned bathrooms. And I positively never cleaned a toilet. That is disgusting. Actually makes me gag. No way would I ever want that as a permanent job. The hardest job is being comfortable talking with Cherish about my feelings or her feelings. Her mother did this so easily. I feel like I'm intruding. I am afraid my daughter will feel less safe with me if I share my painful and frightened feelings with her. How can she depend on a dad who seems to be falling apart?"

Brooksie offers, "Sharing feelings, all kinds of feelings, is not falling apart. You might be surprised if you tell Cherish just how much you are hurting. She may then feel it is okay to talk about fears and hurts."

Justin shares, "I'm practically in the same boat. Marinda, my wife, was the caretaker of her family's emotional lives. Everyone went to her when they were hurting emotionally. If they hurt physically, they more often came to me. Now I am trying, most of the time unsuccessfully, to be mom and dad, at least to Shirley, my youngest.

I am trying to get closer to my youngest daughter and to my grown kids as well. My wife always did all of the birthday and holiday gift buying and party planning. I blew my chance on Shirley's sixteenth birthday, but I am already making plans for a family Christmas party. I'm going to cheat and get some outside help, but I'm going to surprise my offspring with a great party. It's something their mother did, and now it is up to me to try to keep up some of her traditions. I see my role expanding into an event planner."

"Justin, that is so heart-warming to hear about your party plans. Your children are fortunate to have you as their Dad, and I truly believe your wife is smiling down on you, cheering you on," says Mary.

Marshall takes his turn, "I was the practical one, more organized, and pragmatic. Now with Thom gone, I have noticed that when I'm with a group of people who Thom and I use to socialize with, I seem to act more like him. I catch myself saying things I've heard him say. Could I be trying to copy Thom's behaviors? It feels like I'm acting, role playing, and sort of crazy."

Brooksie asks Marshall if he could give specific examples. "For one, I talk a lot more at social gatherings. I'm more animated like Thom. I'm getting involved in a few causes. I've joined an organization called MADD, Mothers Against Drunk Driving. I'm spending a small amount of time volunteering, and sending in some financial support for the organization.

"This one is the strangest. I'm feeding a stray cat that just showed up in my backyard two weeks ago. I tried to shoo it away, ignore it, but with no luck. I know Thom would have fed it, so now I feed it and, of course, the cat is around the house all of the time. What is happening to me?" A slight grin begins to form.

Rachael leans forward and speaks to Marshall, "First, let me assure you that you are not crazy. You're not any crazier than anyone else grieving a devastating loss. Sounds like you have incorporated a few of Thom's interests, and that seems like a good thing to me. He apparently cared for animals and now you have taken that role over of caregiver. Congratulations. I'm sure the cat appreciates your new interest. What an expression of a loving memorial. You loved many things about him, his social skills, his connection with others, and his compassionate heart for all kinds of creatures. Part of his legacy to you was his all embracing heart and now, for a time, you have taken up carrying his torch."

Tears running down his unshaven cheeks, Marshall made no attempt to wipe them away. "I can't say I ever thought my feeding a stray cat so significant, but I like what you said about my carrying his torch. We often teased each other about some of our behaviors. I would accuse him of being a marshmallow, and he would tell me that I am really just a sugar cube and one day tears would melt me."

"Maybe that cat didn't just accidentally find you. Have you named the cat yet," asks Harvey?

"Not really. I'm leaning towards Thomasina. That name seems to fit. She does keep me company in the evening. I let her come in the house, and she rubs against my legs and settles in one of living room chairs. Guess I need to get a litter box."

Harvey continues on with his role changes. "I'm doing laundry now, and the rest of the jobs Helen did for us, shopping, cooking, and cleaning. Helen was ill, very ill, for about one and a half years so I was already doing most of the everyday chores just going through the motions. My role had already been changing, but I still feel like I have experienced an amputation. It feels like my right arm is gone. She was the wind beneath my wings, like the song says. I keep hoping she will send me a sign that she is okay."

Brooksie asks Harvey if he remembers any specific dreams?

"Not usually. I have had a few lately that I remember, but they make no sense to me."

"Can you share them with us?"

"I can try. About a month ago I was dreaming about riding a bike. I knew it was me. I was an adult trying to ride a small tricycle and not doing it very well. My legs were much too long, and I was all twisted up and bent over and trying to peddle. I saw in the distance some person holding a regular bike and I was struggling to get to that person and bike. Then, I woke up."

"Does that dream have any particular meaning for you?" Brooksie asks.

"Well, I sort of knew I had outgrown the tricycle and was trying to grow up. I thought maybe that was Helen encouraging me to move up to the next adventure. She was telling me I was ready. That movement would be easier if I let go of the old and tried the new."

"How do you feel about your dream, and what do you think the message was?" asks Anita.

"The dream left me feeling a little sad, because Helen wasn't riding next to me and I would have to ride on without her. But, just maybe it was Helen letting me know it is time to move on. It's time to change the old for something new that fits better. I don't have to struggle so hard anymore. She may be telling me she is near, and I can go on without her next to me, because she is still with me in spirit."

Kathy, wiping away the wetness on her face, says to Harvey, "Your dream, no, your interpretation of your dream, gives me hope for myself. As far as role changes, Dick was so good at fixing everything, I don't have the slightest idea what to do when something breaks or doesn't work. I didn't even know where the circuit breaker was, so when the electricity went off in the kitchen I didn't have a clue what to do. I wasn't so helpless before I met Dick, it is just that he was so good about doing so many things, and I let myself grow dependent on him."

"What did you do when the electricity went off?" asks Rachael.

"First, I called my neighbors, but they weren't home, so next I called Harvey. He told me exactly where to look and what to do. By the way, Harvey I want to thank you for your help."

"Anytime." He smiles in a way that exudes kindness.

"So it sounds like a problem presented itself, Dick was not there, so you figured out how to get help. A new role for you, and you successfully figured out how to solve the problem."

"Yes, I guess I did. I would like to share one of my dreams. My dream took place near some mountains. The ground was very warm, but getting cooler the further I walked. There was a kid throwing something like hot rocks at me. I kept dodging them, and walking away from the kid all at the same time. I couldn't understand why this stranger was trying to hurt me and I yelled out, 'why?' The word echoed off all the mountains and hurt my ears. I covered my ears and started crying. Next thing I knew I was awake and still crying."

Rachael asks her to think about why she had cried out. "You yelled out why. Why what? What was your question?"

"Maybe I was asking why Dick, why not me, and then I dodged the rocks. Dick didn't. Perhaps I had time to see the danger. I was more cautious than Dick. He was so relaxed and never thought about bad things happening. Guess he was ready to go or stay. Perhaps he had learned what he needed to in this life, and I still need to dodge the bullets. I want to learn how to worry less and live more. That would be a role change for me."

Brooksie says to Kathy, "You wrote down the word volcano, describing your feelings in a previous session. In your dream you were walking away from the hot rock surface and it was getting cooler. It sounds as if you have set a new direction for yourself.

"Our dreams can often be useful messages. They can give us information about ourselves, our feelings and even tell us when we are stuck in one place. Kathy it seems that now you are on the move."

"I am also on the move," interjects Heidi. "Don't know where I'm headed, but I no longer feel stuck in my own anger. I'm not thrashing around in quicksand, barely keeping my head above the mud. My dad was probably trying to get away from himself, his own pain and not from me. Maybe that was what Rolf was doing. They both should have considered what others would feel, but maybe they just couldn't stand one more unbearable moment. I don't ever want to feel like they did. They reached bottom and could see no light, no ladder, no way up, they only saw one way out. What a tragedy, and so many are hurt by one person's actions."

DE-BRIEFING SESSION

Brooksie speaks first. "I know the murders of Ray and maybe of Jim are what we are most concerned about, but let's share our impressions of this session first. I feel a strong need to stay focused on what is going on in group, to stay in the present."

Rachael follows. "It seems Mary mostly listens. She is very supportive of the others. My question is, should we encourage her to share more about herself?"

"Maybe she is getting what she needs from the group simply by listening rather than sharing. How are we to know what she is really feeling about her place in the group?" responds Anita.

"Remember one of our cardinal rules, when in doubt, simply ask. So I suggest we ask Mary herself. We can remind the group about the foolishness of comparing one's loss to another person's loss," Brooksie offers.

Rachael adds, "Mary is a little older, like Justin, from most of the others in the group. They were raised in a culture that expected people to keep their feelings and troubles to themselves, a stiff upper lip kind of tradition. Not everyone needs to share numerous details in order to work through their feelings. Perhaps we could simply ask her if she is getting what she needs from the sessions. We can hear what she says and go from there."

"I want to change the subject, if you two don't mind," says Anita. "Do either of you think those men were murdered or committed suicide?"

"I'm waiting to hear what the police have found out after examining Jim Marcus's body, and if they find something suspicious, then I would definitely consider they both died unwillingly," answers Brooksie.

Anita raises her eyebrows. "I've watched enough cop shows to know that everyone who knew the victim becomes a person of interest. If they do check us out, will they also include Sharon, Curtis, our relatives, maybe even old relationships?"

"Yes, I believe everyone who works at this site will be checked, and the relatives who live close by. Why do you ask?"

"No special reason, just curious. Well, that's not exactly true. Lately I've been uncomfortable around Sharon because she keeps going on and on about the two deaths. I've tried to change the subject by asking how her sister was doing. She has talked about Maureen in the past, and I believe they are very close. Maureen stays with her frequently. I think Sharon has been more like a mother to her, rather than just a sister. Sharon seemed to get irritated with me and told me I was being nosy. That took me by surprise, but I let it go."

"Anita, we are all talking about the deaths. Don't forget, many television shows are exaggerated in the Hollywood style. That includes detective programs."

"Now I'm beginning to wonder if my ex-boyfriend should be investigated," states Rachael. "Maybe I'll speak with one of the detectives about him. I wouldn't want to stir up a hornets nest, but I have an uneasy feeling about Richard. What do you guys think?"

Both of them agree she should talk with the detectives about Richard, if she has any doubts.

CHAPTER XV

The Presence of the absence
Is everywhere.

EDNA ST. VINCENT MILLAY

ONGOING INVESTIGATION

Back at the police department, Detective Swain is holding a file and addressing his partner, Marino. "The report is here, and it confirms our suspicions about Marcus. He tested positive for Zonact as did Sorenson. Both men had traces of alcohol, enough to double the effects of the Zonact. It appears they were both practically unconscious when one was pushed off the boat and the other off the cliff. There is still a slight possibility they could have planned their demise.

"No more question about an accidental death, but it doesn't rule out suicide. Personally, from what the staff, family, co-workers, and one of the neighbors had to say, I can't see either guy doing himself in.

"It seems more than just coincidental that two young men attending grief support groups, at different times, would also die of the same drug. They both had young daughters and were both apparently dating an unknown person. Why would these guys not have introduced their lady friend to their daughters, or to the mother, or mother-in-law? They both apparently dated one person for about two to four months and were probably murdered."

"My gut tells me we are looking for one very disturbed

woman or a sick jealous guy. Could even be two of them, a team. But what the hell is the motive?" questions Marino.

Detective Marino is the man in charge. Even though Swain has more seniority, Marino is the one with the drive and the fine-tuned instincts. Swain seems very comfortable to let the younger man take the lead.

Marino, talking mostly to himself, but also addressing his partner says, "We need to continue asking questions of family, friends, co-workers, neighbors, and anyone else Marcus and Sorensen may have been seeing. We know some of their hobbies. What about secrets? We need names, addresses, and phone numbers of relatives of the deceased wives. Was there any suspicion around the way the wives died? Maybe we are looking for someone who was or is motivated by revenge. Then, there is the staff at the clinic. We'll question everyone, listening for inconsistencies. We also need to look back further to see if anyone else has died who had attended one of their groups when they started the clinic.

"Rudy, why don't you take Sorensen's picture to the marina where he kept his sail boat and see if anyone recognizes him and if they had ever seen him with a women. Also, go to the ranger's station near the mountain where Marcus died. "

Next morning Swain drives out to Mt. Sugar Loaf. He found Ranger Burns in the park office. After introductions were made, the ranger shares what he remembers about Jim Marcus.

Swain shows him a picture of Mr. Marcus. Burns says, "I don't need a photograph because the poor man didn't look much like himself after falling so far, plus he had been dead for awhile. It is the circumstances of the death and the weeks of looking for him and his companion that I most remember. Do you mind if I call in another ranger? She may have more to add."

"Please do," responds Swain.

The ranger calls, Laurie Smith, on her cell phone and asks her to come to the office.

"Ranger Smith will be here in half an hour. Can you wait for her?"

Swain grins. "Gladly, if you have some coffee handy,"

The two chat and drink coffee till Ranger Smith arrives. The detective introduces himself and makes the reason for his visit known.

Laurie Smith tells him of her recollections, "I did see a lone woman walking on the trail marked the Bird Trail, the day that Marcus died. Of course that was before his body was found. She was quite a looker, dark hair covered with a hat. What struck me most was her unfriendliness. I spoke to her, asked her if she had seen any interesting birds on her walk. She seemed in a hurry and barely looked at me. She said she had been hiking alone and was in a hurry to get home."

Swain asked, "Could you give me more of a detailed description of her?"

"Yes, she was much taller than me, and I'm five feet, six inches. She was lean, light skin, almost pale, and she wore a beautiful emerald ring on her right hand. Most of her face was hidden under her straw hat, and she spoke in a low voice, barely audible. She wore some fancy sunglasses. Sorry, that is all I saw of her that day."

"Could you give a description to our department artist, and, hopefully, he can draw us a close likeness of her, with your help?"

"I will do my best."

"By the way, did you happen to notice what kind of car she left in?" Swain asks.

"There were two cars in the lot early that morning. One belonged to Mr. Marcus. We had to have it towed away. The other car was some kind of sports looking car, silver in color, if I'm remembering correctly. I didn't see who drove it away."

The detective thanks both rangers and returns to his car and heads for the marina.

Rudy Swain returns to the office around 5 p.m. He writes up

his reports from the rangers and from the marina. The detective starts the report, "I located one person who had seen Ray Sorenson and a lady the morning of the day he died. His name is Roger Moste, and he told me that she was close to his height of five feet nine inches, long blond hair, great figure, wearing shorts and a skimpy top. Said he didn't really see her face, large sunglasses, type of sun hat, and she kept her head sort of down when he greeted her. She answered back with a quick hello. He did see some kind of scar on her upper thigh and mentioned he couldn't help but notice she had great legs."

"I'm going to notify the clinic that we need to talk with each staff member, one at a time, here at the precinct," said Detective Marino.

"Rudy, you and I will interview the staff, and we need to interview the family members individually in their homes. They should be more at ease in their own surroundings. They've had enough trauma already with the news of murder. It must be much harder to deal with a loved one dying by murder or suicide rather than a natural or accidental death."

Rudy asks, "Do you think we should also ask someone from the Grief Clinic to accompany us as well, support for the families?" A slight upward curve begins at the corner of his lips.

Marino responds, "No. We can't rule out anyone as a suspect yet, that includes the staff of the clinic and the others, in the same building. Plus your suggestion is too easy to see through. You're too big and hairy to be a cupid. Maybe when this investigation is over with and we have the bad guy, bad girl, or whoever the perk is, I will make a call."

"Why don't you ask Brooksie out for coffee one time. I have seen you looking at her. I know that look. I've had that look myself a time or two," adds Swain.

"Don't play the match game with me, Rudy. I hate to be pushed. Reminds me of what my folks pull. Every time I go home

I get the third degree about plans for my future. Mom just blurts out, 'time to settle down and give me grandchildren.'"

Back at the clinic Melissa is answering the phone. "Brooksie, Detective Marino is calling and don't be so standoffish. I think he has a thing for you. I've seen that glint in a guy's eye before, and I know what it means. You start taking giant steps backwards anytime someone seems in the least bit interested."

"Thanks for your motherly observations, but I am just fine as I am. Hello, detective, what can I do for you?"

"The toxicology reports are both finished and in the files. I'm now at liberty to say that accidental death for either man is no longer a possibility. Your office will soon be getting a call from Swain or me, setting up individual interviews. The interviews will need to be held at the police station."

Brooksie's complexion pales and she asks, "Do you think there is any chance that any of our clients could be at risk? I'm becoming frightened and wondering if the offices should be closed. There are one or two clients that have similar circumstances like Ray and Jim. They are both widowers and have young daughters. I am becoming concerned for them. Are you going to tell the families of the dead men, about your suspicions? I feel like I'm running around in a pitch black room, with no flashlight. What can be told to the staff, the clients in therapy or those involved in group sessions. What do we say to the relatives of the two deceased men, if they ask us questions, and they will? I know I'm rambling on, but I feel strongly about protecting our clientele."

"I hear your concerns. You can't give answers to questions that you don't know, and neither can I. Our department needs a great deal more information, and it will take time. If we need more help with phone calls and leg work, we will request it from our division. We want a list of all of the widowers who were or are fairly young, and have young children, who have been enrolled in a grief support group, in the past three to four years. Same goes for anyone fitting that description who is attending a group right now. I can get you court orders for those names and their files, just say the word."

"Send me the order and I will have our secretary get that information to you, as soon as possible." responds Brooksie.

The minute she hangs up the phone, she quickly dials the lawyer, who has been advising the staff. They set up an evening appointment for Friday. All or any of the therapists, psychologists, volunteers and secretary will be invited and encouraged to attend. *Confidentiality can be a pain in the backside when complicated by homicide. I should have listened to my aunt and studied to be a veterinarian or to my precious uncle and become an exotic dancer.*

CHAPTER XVI

No matter how bad your heart is broken the
world doesn't stop for your grief.

AUTHOR UNKNOWN

SESSION EIGHT
STRESS AND MANAGEMENT

Brooksie thinking to herself, *I certainly hope no one from any of*
the grief groups has seen the short article on the inside page of the
local paper. They all have enough on their plates at the moment.

No such luck. The group is assembling and sounding like a
beehive, everybody talking at once. From what is being said, the
murders are taking center stage.

Brooksie comments, "I am assuming most of you have heard
something about the mysterious deaths of two men who had
attended different grief groups here. The staff does not know
any more than was written in the brief article in the newspaper.
The police have been speaking to us, gathering information. As
you know, we have privacy issues, an obligation to protect all
clients, and we are doing that. If and when we learn any more
that is relevant to their deaths or to the grief clinic, we certainly
will do our best to keep you informed. We are as much in the
dark as you all are."

Rachael begins, "Now let us bring our focus back to today.
My question is to you, Mary. Are you receiving what you need
from this group? You are supportive of everyone. You are a very
sensitive listener and often offer wise and caring feedback. I

wonder if you feel you must minimize your grief because you compare your circumstances with other group members?"

"I don't believe I have been minimizing my feelings. I miss Sam terribly, but I had many fine years with him.

"Growing older requires acceptance of all kinds of losses including death of loved ones, and even of oneself. If I had had a choice, Sam and I would have both died in our sleep, the same night, when we would be in our late nineties. That is, if we both still enjoying reasonable health, our families, and life in general.

"But, that is not the way of the world. I have been working for many years and have been involved with death many times over. I am used to listening to others, but that doesn't mean I'm ignoring myself. I have been able to identify at one time or another with everyone in the room. This group has taught me a great deal about tolerance and compassion. I look forward to our sessions every week and will feel a little sad when they end."

Dell asks, "Do you, or, actually, do any of you think you will ever have another romantic relationship again, dating, maybe even marriage?"

Rachael responds, "That's an interesting question, Dell. Do you think you will ever date again and maybe even fall in love? How do you think your daughter will feel if you do start a new relationship?"

"I can't imagine ever putting myself in the position of being so deeply hurt again. I'm embarrassed to say this, but lately I have missed our sex life. We were so compatible in all areas of our togetherness. To answer your question, Rachael, about my daughter's feelings, I don't know what she will feel about another woman in her father's life. At the moment that is not a concern for either of us."

"I would give that some serious thought," responds Rachael.

Anita offers, "Only seems natural that your daughter's well-being is on your mind and it also sounds natural for you to miss making love to your wife. Remember though, your daughter will be grown up and ready to be on her own in the not-so-far-off future. Your treatment of her now will forever be burned into her memory bank."

"I don't think about intimacy often, but when I do, I feel like a traitor to my wife and guilty as hell. Anita, I am painfully aware of how important my behaviors are to Cherish. I just hope there will be some balance in both our lives sooner than later."

Justin speaks, "I think it is a waste of time to feel guilty about our natural instincts. Sex is so basic a need. It reminds us we are still among the living."

Rachael responds, "How do each of you attempt to manage the natural callings of nature or whatever causes you stress."

"Well," responds Dell, "I usually take my daughter to the tennis courts and we play until we are both pretty worn out. The activity seems to help us release or relieve our pent up emotions. I need activity and so does she. When I'm not at my job, then, she and I do something together, tennis, swim, yard or house work, or play video games. We go to the movies every week. We also eat out quite a bit."

"Dell, are you sleeping any better?" asks Anita.

"Oh yes. I get almost five to six hours at night, much better than two months ago when I could barely get two to three hours broken up, if I was lucky."

"Your daughter is fortunate that you spend so much time with her," replies Kathy. Rachael agrees with her.

Harvey looks at Dell, "Rachael is right, but don't forget you have adult needs and she has needs of a child. Both are legitimate. My wife and I weren't intimate for almost a year. She was too sick and in too much pain. I just didn't have those thoughts. How could I when she was so sick and was suffering? With that said, I now find my interest has returned. I see that as a good thing. One day I hope to start dating again. Helen told me she didn't want me to pine away. She said I had made her so happy, and it would be just fine with her if I would eventually make another lady as happy."

"Sounds like you had a wonderful, unselfish wife. She gave you permission, even encouraged you to find another partner, eventually. Your wife wanted you to be happy. Now that is true love in my book," adds Mary.

There was a pause, then Kathy chimes in. "I do feel really stressed out. The hoodlums who killed my Dick are going to be in court next week for the third time. I can't seem to stay away, but I get so worked up in the court room just seeing the faces of those two murderers. How dare they be alive while my Dick is six feet underground.

"One of the killers was injured by the police, and his lawyer has the nerve to say that his client is not receiving adequate medical attention. That rat killed one innocent bystander and seriously wounded another, and he has the nerve, the right to complain about anything? Our justice system stinks. I'm screaming inside, and yet, if I were to say anything, I would be asked to leave the court room. Where the hell is justice and fairness? The bad guys lost their rights when they took away the life of another. What is the matter with our courts? I can hardly breathe when I think about our justice system. Horrible people have more rights than the good ones. I'm not supposed to voice my complaints in court, but the asshole who murdered the love of my life can have his complaints aired in the courtroom. This is justice?"

The room feels instantly charged. Intense emotions radiate from Kathy and pass from one member to another.

Brooksie says, "I definitely understand your anger and frustrations, so I offer my validation. Your grief is complicated by outside events not under your control; dealing with the lawyers, court processes, actually seeing and hearing the perpetrators who murdered your husband is all so overwhelming. You may even be bothered by reporters and curiosity seekers. These challenges can go on for quite a long time. It is in your best interest to bring in as much support as you need from trusted and reliable friends. You may even find some friends step away from you. Murder is scary to all and involvement may seem threatening. Isolation will also increase your stress and anxiety. Your grief work is daunting, but not impossible."

"Kathy, you know you can call me anytime," offers Heidi.

The group members tell Kathy how available they are to her, day and night. Each member reminds her about the group being a family, bonded by grief.

Rachael asks, "Do you feel it is good for you to go to the court hearings?"

"I have mixed feelings. I tell myself I won't go to the next hearing, but, when the day arrives, I feel drawn and almost unable to stop myself from attending the session."

Brooksie asks Kathy, "What do you think will happen at the hearing if you don't go?"

"Those two bastards, the judge, the lawyers, and the bastards' families will forget that Dick meant something special to someone. If I don't go, then Dick is like a ghost, invisible, and unable to speak for himself. I need to stand up and speak for him."

She puts her head down and begins to sob, her whole upper body moving in tandem with each outcry. "I'm beginning to forget what he smelled like; the sound of his voice, and especially his smile. I feel like I am losing my mind. I lose a part of him with each passing day."

Brooksie continues, "Your world has been turned upside down and inside out, nothing makes sense, nothing in it is in the right place. Grief is crazy making, and the murder of a beloved mate by strangers is truly crazy, unbelievable, but this is what you are being asked to do, to accept the fact the Dick is dead, he is not returning. He was randomly murdered by strangers for a small amount of money. You are being forced to adjust and accept whatever our legal system does to the two murderers and you have no voice, no control. You are being asked to go on, not only remain with the living, but to thrive in this life without the most important person who had been in your world. No, you are not crazy. You are courageous for trying to do what feels impossible, but is necessary for your own survival. To honor Dick's life and his love for you is the task you have before you."

Marshall struggles to talk because of the catch in his throat. He cradles his head in his large hands. He finally manages to say, "Thank God someone else feels like I do. I have evil thoughts towards the drunk who killed Thom. Not a day goes by that I don't think about revenge. I want him to suffer just like me. Thom was worth a thousand of those drunken drivers.

"Sometimes I think I will never be at peace until the driver dies, and I want his death to be prolonged and painful. I know I sound hateful and horrible, but that fantasy sometimes gives me strength to get through the day.

"I also have gone to the courthouse. I stare at Mr. Placer. I feel like I'm torturing myself by sitting in the same room with him, but I want to see him held accountable. I feel crazy with revenge and hate at times. For my own health I need to, somehow, stop thinking about payback, but the fact is, I don't want to. Forgiveness seems way beyond me at this time."

Marshall takes a deep breath. "I was thinking about your question, Brooksie. What do I think would happen if I didn't go to the courthouse? I think I might lose some of my anger. But, I believe I need the anger to keep myself going day to day. I have noticed that, when I share any of my feelings with this group, the rest of the day goes a lot better. Guess we will have to stay connected until all of us are in a better place."

Justin shares some insights, "In the past, I have shied away from continuing relationships with patients. I am rethinking this behavior and attitude. No wonder some of them tried to keep a friendship going with me. They had had life changing experiences and I was a part of it. I sure missed the boat."

DE-BRIEFING SESSION

Sharon and Curtis ask if they might join the de-briefing session. They both say they have concerns and questions about the investigation of the probable homicides.

Sharon's appears tired, dark circles under her eyes and her face is drawn. She says, "I am wondering if we need to be cautious? Do the police think any of us are in danger, or surely they are not thinking of us as suspects?"

"I didn't get the impression that we were suspects. I think their questioning of each one of us, at the police station, is simply routine. As far as being in danger, I believe the detectives would inform us, if we were in harms way," says Rachael.

"I've had a few nightmares lately," says Anita. They wake me up, but I can't remember much of the dream, except I'm running slowly. I can't seem to go very fast and I have no idea what I'm running from. Sharon, remember I told you last week about this upsetting dream that I had several times?"

Not waiting for Sharon to answer, Anita continues, "In fact, you also shared a dream of yours, or maybe it was your sister's dream. I can't remember whose dream it was. It was about a disfigured adult and a child. The child was pushed into a small boat and pushed out into the water. She was all alone and terrified, crying out for help, but no one came."

Sharon closes her eyes and pushes her glasses up higher on her nose, "Vaguely, but, yes, I do. That dream was my sister's dream. She has struggled with abandonment issues since our mother died. Many others have these same issues after a parent dies, abandons, or neglects them, especially, if they are young when the parent dies."

She continues, "My stress level is climbing higher every

day. Are the police offering any information? There must be something we can do to help? Brooksie, do you know anymore?"

"According to the detectives, information about any suspects is scarce. It is my understanding there is a fairly large police workforce trying to identify and apprehend the culprits. There is a network of people involved gathering facts. Interviewing is just one part of the job. Marino and Swain are simply in charge of the crime team. Their investigation is detail oriented and takes time. I think they are trying hard to find answers."

After a short silence, Virginia speaks up. "I do remember something that Ray Sorensen said about his lady friend. The lady said she understood his daughter's concerns, because her own mother had died when she was quite young. Now I wonder, if that was true, why didn't she make more of an effort to get acquainted with his daughter? They had something in common."

Curtis is nervously moving around in his chair, "Maybe that was too close for comfort for her. Perhaps she still had some issues left over from her past. Guess we will never know unless she shows up."

Lucinda says that Dan and she had been talking about Jim Marcus.

Dan nods, "Marcus told me in private, well, as private as a conversation can be at a grocery store, how physically turned on he was by his new friend. He said she was very exciting and very intense, in fact, so intense it frightened him a little, but excited him at the same time."

They all chat for a while longer, many questions and few answers. Everyone leaves except Brooksie and Anita.

Brooksie asks Anita if she had time to join her for a cup of coffee at the coffee house down the street.

Anita answers with an affirmative nod, causing her long, curly hair to dance up and down.

Together they walk down the street to the coffee house. They find a table, in the corner, and order their specialty coffees.

Brooksie says, "Anita, I didn't realize that you and Sharon socialize."

"Oh yes. She calls me to go to a movie or lunch once in awhile. It's not like we are good friends or anything. Actually I'm flattered that someone so smart wants to spend a little time with me. Not sure why she does, but I always say yes and have a good time, and she always picks up the bill, saying she makes more than I do. That is definitely true. One time she even invited me to her house for lunch. You know, she has quite an office at home. She has a bunch of filing cabinets for her research. Sharon is compiling information on the effects of parental loss on children. She plans to write books on the subject. Her main interest is following the child after the parental loss to adulthood. Sharon is considering, *How Could You Leave Me*, as a possible title. She told me she keeps all her notes locked in filing cabinets in her home office.

"Sharon encourages me to continue my education. She even told me she thinks I'll make an excellent psychologist. I think she sees herself as my mentor, which truly pleases me."

"Have you ever met her sister?" I ask.

"No. Sharon says her sister, Maureen, has a very busy life. That she dates a great deal and keeps her personal life to herself." Anita adds, "Sharon mentioned if she asks Maureen about her private life, she gets irritated with her and reminds her that she is not her mother. Sharon stated to me that, she actually feels like her mother, because she did much of the caregiving when they were growing up. She also told me that Maureen can be quite a handful at times, very moody and has trouble sleeping. Mothering is a hard habit to break. I should know because I'm also telling my brother what he should or should not do. Sharon seems very devoted to her sister, sort of the way I am with my brother."

CHAPTER XVII

*"Happiness is beneficial for the body but it is grief
that develops the powers of the mind."*

MARCEL PROUST
REMEMBRANCE OF THINGS PAST:
THE PAST RECAPTURED

INTERVIEWS OF STAFF

Dan and Lucinda arrive together at the police station and are
ushered into Detective Marino's office. Swain stood holding the
door for the rest.

Marino asks Lucinda to have a seat in the waiting area and
then motions Dan into the office and reminds Dan the interview
will be recorded.

"No problem," says Dan.

Swain begins the interview. "Please state your name, address,
age, if you are married, and if you have children living at home."

"My name is Dan Potter, 5005 Maple Street, age fifty, married
yes, for ten years to Roanna, two children from my previous
marriage. I have a son and a daughter, eighteen and twenty, not
living at home."

"You were one of the social workers in charge of the grief
support group that Jim Marcus attended for twelve weeks?"

"Yes."

"Do you remember anything unusual happening in any of
the sessions?"

"No. Not really. Though I do believe that Mr. Marcus was

interested in Lucinda, the social worker, although that is not so unusual, as she is a beautiful woman and he was single, a widower. She is also single and has received her share of attention. In fact, Lucinda mentioned to me and to Sharon about Marcus, I did call him and remind him that staff and clients are not to get involved during the twelve weeks of sessions. He always stayed after the session, and tried to talk to her alone. It is our policy that two staff members always remain to the last. In Lucinda's case, I waited nearby while they visited and then I walked her to her car. After night sessions end, I'm always cautious with our female staff."

Swain nods and makes a note, "Did Ms. Chavez, Lucinda, make a complaint or seem concerned about the attention Mr. Marcus paid her? She is a beautiful woman. Many men would be attracted to her. Even a married man, like you, for instance, might find her attractive."

"Well, even if I have been married a long time, it doesn't mean I'm blind. Our office has quite a few good lookers. But we all maintain our professionalism. No, she never complained about him."

"How would you characterize your relationship with your wife? Great, okay, some rough edges or not so good?"

"I just said we all maintain our professional roles. My marriage is great and so is my job. You are not thinking that someone at the clinic has anything to do with these deaths, are you?"

"These questions are just routine, Dan. Did you ever see Jim Marcus after the sessions were completed?"

"Yes, as a matter of fact, I ran into him in the mall and another time in a grocery store. We spoke briefly. His daughter was with him. He told me that she was going to counseling and that they were both doing just fine. That was about two to three months after his last session with Lucinda, Virginia, and me."

"Did he ask about Lucinda?"

"No, but he did ask about Anita. He wanted to know if it would be alright for him to call her, at the office, for a coffee type date. I told him the clinic frowns on any romantic kind of socializing between clients and staff; at least, for one year after their last session. That is just an unwritten policy we have decided upon. Seems like a good idea to me."

"Thank you, Dan. If you think of anything else, no matter how insignificant, please give us a call."

Lucinda is ushered into the office next, and she's reminded about the taping of the interview.

"My name is Lucinda Chavez. I am thirty-one and live at 1441 March Street. I am single and glad of it. I have no children. Yes, it is okay to tape this interview. I do remember being told about the taping."

Detective Marino interviews Lucinda. "What do you remember about the sessions with Jim Marcus?"

"He was a nice looking man, always looked fit and immaculately groomed. He was very upset and tearful the first month and then he seemed to be learning to live with the death of his wife, slowly adjusting."

"Did he ever seem overly friendly to you or other staff members?"

"What do you mean? Oh, Dan has been talking out of turn again. Mr. Marcus did ask me to go for coffee with him. I said no, and told him that socializing with a new widower was inappropriate and would not be beneficial. He said he understood, but he did ask me one more time toward the end of the twelve weeks. Again, I said no. To which he politely responded, 'Okay, just had to try again.' I shared the fact he was a little persistent with Sharon, Dan, and Virginia. Dan told me he didn't think it so unusual for a widower to be interested in dating sooner than a widow. He added there is a bond that develops with the facilitators and the mourners. So it makes sense the male feels drawn to the female therapists. Months later, I learned he had called Anita and asked for a date. She also said no, and gave the same reasons I had. That was the last time I heard anything about Jim. That is, until now. What a tragedy, especially for his daughter."

Detective Marino continues, "Do you think Dan Potter has a romantic interest in you?"

"I think he is a hopeless romantic and also a gentleman. He is a wonderful facilitator and always acts professionally with all the women here. I do think, on his own time, he may have a wandering eye, but my gut feeling is, he just likes to look. He seems happily married. He speaks often and well of his wife."

"I have one more question for you. What outdoor hobbies do you have?"

"I like swimming, preferably in a pool, except on hot days, and then I go to the ocean. I do walk a few miles most every day and work out at a gym three days a week."

Rachael is next to be interviewed, and the same instructions were given to her. She stated she had no first-hand knowledge of Mr. Marcus, that she had never met the man and he never called her.

Detective Swain asks, "Have you ever dated Dan Potter?"

"What! He is married and, also, even more important, he is a colleague. Did he say we had?"

"No, he did not."

Rachael went on to say, "Dan fancies himself a lady's man. He is probably all talk, but no go. I think he has had a crush on Lucinda for quite awhile, but he likes his career too much to really get involved. Plus, I think he truly loves his wife. She is a great gal and seems to understand his flirtatious nature. Wish I could be more like her. I do think he gets a little possessive of the women at the office. Actually, he casually flirts with all of us. Dr. Primm is the only one who gets angry with him. The rest of us take him with a grain of salt."

"Before we finish up, please tell me if you have any hobbies and what they are."

"I like lots of sports. I love to water ski, will go sailing with anyone who asks me to, and I have done my share of hiking in the nearby mountains. Brooksie and I play a pretty mean game of tennis every so often. I also love to dance. I go skiing in the winter as often as I can find time. Last year, almost all of us from the clinic went on a three day skiing trip together."

Next to be interviewed is Anita.

Anita gives the requested information and is then asked basically the same interview questions. "I do remember Jim Marcus. He came on to Lucinda and to me. He did gracefully accept no and didn't seem offended. Grief affects everyone a little differently. He was missing his wife and bed partner. He worked hard at being both mother and father to his daughter. Naturally, he did have his own physical needs. That is certainly normal. If I hadn't been involved with him in a professional way I would have probably gone on a date with him."

Detective Marino asks "We understand Dan Potter is quite the lady's man. Has he ever shown a jealous side to you? For example, did he seem overly concerned about the attention Marcus paid to you or Lucinda?"

"Oh, he is a harmless flirt, but he is most definitely excellent in a group situation, compassionate and insightful. He has a good heart for all those who are in mourning. And no, I have never gotten the feeling that he was jealous of anyone. I think he simply feels protective of the ladies of the staff. I know Sharon gets irritated with him, but she acts rather old fashioned and gets stuffy at times with everyone."

"One last question, do you like to sail or to hike in the mountains?"

"Sure, I like the water. I haven't done much sailing, but I have hiked with my brother on Mount Hood a few times. I have done some snow skiing, but I'm not very good. Why?"

"The questions are just routine, Anita. Thanks for your help and cooperation."

Anita is dismissed and Detective Marino asks Dan to return to the interview room.

When Dan walks in he says, "Oh boy, my wife always tells me my flirtatious nature will get me into trouble one day."

"You're not in trouble. I just want to know how you get along with Sharon Primm? Have you ever been at odds with her?"

"Yes. We had a disagreement about her sister. Sharon felt I was being too nosey. That was only a one time occurrence. I realized I had overstepped my place. Sharon is a very private person and doesn't talk about herself or her family. Sharon used to have a picture of her sister and herself on her desk. It was taken when they were teenagers. Last time I was in her office, awhile back, I noticed she had apparently removed it. Her sister is a few years younger. They both looked to be beauties in their youth, and Sharon is still a knockout. So I imagine her sister is also still gorgeous. Sharon doesn't capitalize on her great looks. Her eyeglasses and some of her outfits aren't very flattering. I have never brought up conversation regarding her sister again. Sharon is an excellent therapist. I have great respect for her, and I have tried never to invade her privacy again."

Virginia is the next one to be questioned.

Detective Swain begins the interview. "Virginia, please tell us what you remember of Ray Sorensen. I understand that you, Brooksie Everett, and Rachael Young were the facilitators in the group he attended."

Virginia gives the required information about name and so forth and begins, "Ray Sorensen was cooperative, didn't say much in the beginning sessions, but warmed up to the group and group process rather quickly. He had no trouble talking about missing his wife, and spoke fondly of his daughter and mother-in-law. I saw him one time after his group had terminated. He was speaking with Melissa, our secretary. He gave me the high sign. He looked quite tan and fit."

"Do you remember if he ever spoke of a lady friend? My second question is about you personally, do you like to sail?"

"No to both questions. Why are you asking me about sailing?"

"Routine questions that we are asking everyone. Thanks for your help and cooperation."

When Melissa's is seated next, she answers that she doesn't remember Jim Marcus. When she is told that Virginia remembers seeing Jim talking with her after his twelve week sessions were completed, she says she still didn't remember him, until she was shown a picture of him. Then her response is, "Oh, yes, he was asking about wanting his daughter to see someone because she was having some problems. I referred him to Dr. Mary Reichlund. Dr. Rey's appointment book was full for several months ahead. Per Dr. Rey's suggestion, I called and made an appointment for the daughter with Dr. Reichlund. That was the last time I saw him."

Detective Swain asks her, "Did Mr. Marcus or Mr. Sorensen ever ask you out?"

"Why would you want to know that?"

"Any information, no matter how trivial it might seem on the surface, might help us."

"Yes, Mr. Sorensen did ask me to go sailing with him one time. I said I would like to, but office policy discourages dating with clients, at least for one year after the client's visits have terminated. He never called me again. Plus, as I said, I wasn't really into sailing. I am not much of an outdoor person. I do like to swim, but I would rather just lie on the beach, read a good book, and stare at the waves. I do love to dance."

"Who else did Ray or Jim ask out, that you are aware of?"

"Lucinda and Anita both said Mr. Marcus had asked them for a date and both women turned down the offers. All members of the staff at the clinic are very professional. It is understood that there is to be no dating with clients or even with other staff members, for a period of time."

"Do you know if he asked Sharon Primm on a date?"

"She never said anything to me, but she is a rather private person. She doesn't talk much about her private life."

It is Sharon's turn to be questioned. Detective Swain begins, "What can you tell us about the two victims, Sharon. Do you mind if I call you by your first name?"

"No. I don't mind what name you call me by. I notice you refer to both dead men as victims, so does that mean you know they were definitely murdered?"

"At this moment all the evidence does point to foul play. We are doing our job which entails collecting all necessary information. Building a case for the courts is detail work. We would appreciate any and all help you and other staff members will give us."

"Sorry, I didn't know either gentleman."

"It is our understanding that Jim Marcus was busy asking several of the ladies from the office on dates. Did he ever ask you for a date?" The detective leaned over the table to show Sharon pictures of Mr. Marcus and Mr. Sorensen.

She looks over the pictures for a long minute then, says, "No, neither man asked me out. We have a mutual agreement between the clinic, Dr. Rey, and me that we do not date clients. It would be unethical and unprofessional. At least, not while they are clients and for a year or so more after they are last seen. My practice is focused on abused women and I don't date women."

"So, then, you would have never seen the daughters of Mr. Sorensen or Mr. Marcus, is that correct?"

"That is correct. Dr. Rey's practice is mostly with the young. I do believe he saw both daughters for a short time and referred one or both to Dr. Mary Reichlund."

"I understand you have a sister."

"What does my sister have to do with your investigation?"

"She probably has nothing at all to do with it, but it is our job to inquire about any and all parties. To your knowledge, did either man have any contact with her? By the way, what is her name and how can we get in touch with her?"

"Maureen Primm is her name. She has her own home, but often stays with me. We have always been very close. I can give you her cell phone number."

"Neither of you married?"

"That is correct." Sharon writes down Maureen's phone number and address and hands it over to the detective.

The interview is over and Brooksie is told her "turn at bat" will be tomorrow. The interviews had taken longer than expected.

Before the therapists and secretary exit the building, the detectives ask them to bring in, or call in, the details of where they were the days that Mr. Marcus and Mr. Sorensen died. "We have the dates fairly well pinned down," replies Swain. "The ranger was able to pinpoint the day the Mr. Marcus was hiking and didn't return to his car. We also have the approximate time that Mr. Sorenson went into the water." The detective hands each person a sticky note with the dates in question.

Detective Swain adds, "We will be asking everyone the same questions and we do check up on all responses."

The next day, Brooksie arrives at the station at the appointed time. The detectives apologize for taking up so much of her time, but explain that investigative work is slow, and tedious, often is responsible for many inconveniences. The interview begins with Brooksie giving the required information about name and so forth. Detective Marino asks her about outdoor hobbies and where had she been on the dates when Mr. Marcus fell to his death and Mr. Sorenson fell off his boat. He tells her there are witnesses who saw Sorensen with a woman the day he died.

Her interview is like the others. She gives her personal impressions and observations of both ex-clients. She tells the detective that neither man had asked her out. She stated her hobbies are collecting unwanted pets, thanks to her aunt, loves to dance, plays tennis, and reads mystery novels. At the end of the interview, Brooksie says she will find her date book and call back with the requested information of her whereabouts.

Brooksie returns to the office and Melissa shows her the court orders for the files and notes on the names listed.

Brooksie addressing Lucinda, Rachael and Dan says, "Here is the list of all the male clients under the age of fifty who had been in a grief support group in the last four years. Let's divide the names up into four lists. Each one of us will call the names on their respective list."

After all calls have been completed, to the relief of therapists, all ex-clients are alive and accounted for.

Melissa makes a phone call to the detectives to let them know the results of the calls pertaining to past grief group clients.

Detective Swain says to Melissa, "Please remind everyone about the information we need about their whereabouts on the dates of the deaths. Someone from the department will be contacting family members, friends, and neighbors. I don't want to give the impression we are focusing on anyone in particular. No matter what you have seen on television, police work is slow, meticulous, and follows a routine. We follow many leads to dead ends."

Later that day, several of the staff members get together at their favorite coffee shop. Lucinda speaks about how her Dad had hurt her by leaving the family. She seems to blame her divorces on her father's abandonment. She says that trust is a huge issue for her especially when it comes to romantic relationships. She speaks about her very demanding mother who blames her for the father leaving them. The group discusses how odd it is that so many of the staff lost a parent at a young age. It is no mystery there is an abundance of concern for the daughters of the two deceased men. Many of the staff members can relate due to their own experiences when they were young.

Anita shares she and her brother had a fairly rough time growing up after their mother's death. She adds that even Sharon and her sister struggle with their mother's death. "The focus of Sharon's research for her book is parental loss for children and how the losses continue to affect them right into adulthood," says Anita.

Sharon approaching the table asks, "What about my sister?" with a penetrating glance at Anita.

"Hi, Sharon. We have been commiserating about our difficult childhoods, which began after the death of a mother. I was saying that even you had some problems or, actually, your sister has apparently been more affected by the death of your mother than you are."

"Yes, that's for sure. I came to terms with the loss of our mother long ago. Our dad was selfish and stupid. I've had no contact with him for years and have no plans to change that. Maureen was younger when mom died, and I think it was more traumatic for her. Since I was older and Dad was so worthless, I became the mother figure. Actually, I still try to mother her. You are sort of in the same boat, Anita. You have taken care of your brother, Brad, since your mother passed on."

"That's true. I do love my brother, but it is quite a responsibility and hasn't left me much time for a private life," answers Anita.

"I wholeheartedly agree," says Sharon. "Maureen acts very carefree, dates a lot and is extremely outgoing. I, on the other hand, take life very seriously, probably too seriously."

Virginia adds her two cents, "My father died when I was thirty-two, and my mother began exhibiting signs of Alzheimers years before he left. Even though I have not had to raise any siblings, I do feel very much like an orphan, a rather empty, alone feeling. I guess you and Sharon might also feel like orphans."

"Since we are actually talking about ourselves, I might as well jump in also," says Rachael. "My wonderful Mom died when I was ten, and Dad was doing an okay job as a single parent. That is, until he married the horrible witch from the west two years after Mom died. I left home at seventeen, married a jerk, and was divorced at twenty. It is easy to see how we all gravitated toward the helping profession. Some of us work with children and some of us have become advocates for the adult walking wounded. Can't believe I eventually picked such a rotten boyfriend. Richard makes my dad look like a saint."

Brooksie asks Rachael, "Have you told the detectives anything about Richard's difficult behaviors?

"Not yet. I will tell them about him when I call and give them the dates they requested from us," answers Rachael. I have to admit I dread telling them about Richard. If Richard finds out I may find myself in a world of hurt. He can get pretty nasty."

"When you talk with the detectives, be sure you mention your fears of retaliation to them," suggests Sharon.

Leaning forward Brooksie says, "I'm sorry about switching the focus here, but I can't imagine why anyone would want to harm Jim or Ray. They both were devoted to their daughters, and had emotional support and assistance from family. The motives for the murders, if they truly were murdered, are a mystery. There is no way it could be someone whom we all know. That is simply impossible in my book. Surely the police can't think for a moment any one of us could do something so horrible."

"You mean you think the police are looking at us as possible suspects?" asks Virginia. She looks surprised.

"Yes," says Brooksie. She looks around the room and adds, "The coffee shop is filling up and since the voice level at our table is increasing, I'm concerned others will overhear us. I think we need to move on. Our conversations are becoming too interesting to those four sitting close to us. We can talk more privately this weekend. Remember, it is party time at my house."

On her way home after leaving the coffee shop, Brooksie runs through a short check list in her head, of what she knows about each one. *Rachael is very passionate about abused kids. She had a difficult time in her teen years. Her stepmom treated her badly and I know she has shared a little of her anger at her dad for allowing the stepmom to be so mean to her. She doesn't seem to make wise choices when it comes to men. Richard sounds controlling and volatile.*

Sharon and her sister lost their mother when they were very young. She is fairly closed-mouth about anything personal.

Even Virginia feels like an orphan. She was older when her dad died, but her mother developed Alzheimers, leaving Virginia basically parentless.

Then there is Lucinda, who is also very private. She is fun to be with and often displays a fiery temperament. She has been divorced twice. No children. She specializes with families. I believe she lives near her mother and that her mother drives her crazy.

There are so many motherless women, all working at the clinic. I wonder how many of them have unresolved issues connected to their parental losses. I know that many therapists are attracted to this specific area of counseling, grief and loss. Perhaps, because it helps them to work through their own mine fields of unresolved loss. Sadly, some are unaware of their own needs, issues, and motives.

A man could also be involved in the deaths. Dan lost his Mother when he was fifteen, and he says he and his Dad are estranged.

Hatred and resentment of a father who abandons his young children would be a motive for some kind of payback.

Enough already. Time to focus on my party. My dear neighbors insist on taking charge of the event. They are special friends to me. This is my third time to host the staff party at the end of summer. Actually, I love having everyone over to my house and showing off my loving pet companions.

Brooksie's home is nestled between tall evergreens and weeping willows on an acre, completely fenced in. She enjoys the wide open kitchen, dining and living area plus the great patio. It has a wrap-around porch plus a built-in outdoor barbeque. The chain link fence is practically invisible covered by creeping vines. *I can't say I earned this great place by the sweat of my brow, because I didn't. I'm so grateful for the generous inheritance. Wish I could thank my benefactor, but he is long ago dead.*

The party.

Lucinda, Dan, and his wife arrive together, soon followed by Anita and Sharon.

Brooksie's neighbors, David and Rolland are the perfect hosts. They make everyone feel special, spoiled, and important. They keep the food and drinks coming almost effortlessly.

Virginia brings a distinguished looking gentleman. Rachael also brings a date, surprising the rest of us. She introduces Mark Latham as a newly found old friend. "We lived next door to each other as kids. We use to play together and with other neighborhood kids."

Curtis arrives half an hour late, apologizing, saying he had been tied up at work.

Aunt Tilly and Uncle Joe were the last to arrive. Broooksie's aunt moves like a tornado throughout the room. She introduces Brooksie's pets to each and everyone, telling them how wonderful her niece is for giving a loving home to dogs and cats abused by horrible people.

By the end of the evening she will have names and phone numbers of possible foster homes for some animals, thinks Brooksie to herself. *A foster home, for Auntie, is the code word for a permanent home.*

Conversation easily flows with the added incentive of wine and good food. There is soft music in the background and the fireplace was crackling. Laughter and lightheartedness fills the living area. Everyone has been under such a strain lately. The offices are overflowing with tension, anxiety, and fear. These few hours are a much needed diversion.

Dan, of course, makes the rounds, dancing with every woman. He appears giddy surrounded by his harem. His wife doesn't seem in the least bit upset with the attention he pays to others. She sort of floats around the room conversing with all she comes in contact with. She appears especially involved in conversations with David and Rolland.

The best dancers in the room are David and Rolland, Brooksie knowing this in advance, is taking advantage and dancing her legs off, rotating between them, that is, until the others realize what great dance partners the two men actually are. After that, Brooksie hardly squeezes in another turn on the dance floor.

A good time is had by all. Sharon is the first to leave, excusing herself because of a headache. Anita isn't ready to leave, so she asked Curtis if he could drop her off at her house later.

It was great fun just watching friends and coworkers relax, enjoy each other's company, and getting to know a little more about the personal side of each one.

Close to 1:00 a.m. people are getting ready to go home. While getting on coats, everyone thanks Brooksie, David, and Rolland. Curtis and Anita were in deep conversation, Brooksie gently reminds them of the time. Her great neighbors were quietly picking up dishes and other remnants of the party.

Anita speaks up, "Curtis and I have been talking about Lucinda and Sharon. They have both been asking a lot of questions about the two men who died. Sharon asks me about our support group now. She has been asking me very personal questions about the members and their families. She says she is interested in what kind of support they have after the twelve sessions are finished. Is it okay for me to talk to her about the members of our group, Brooksie?"

"No, not by individual names. Sharon is a well-qualified psychologist and is often writing articles on different subjects. I believe she is always keeping her ears open for research purposes and to further her own knowledge and skills. She has told several of us she is working on a book having to do with the effects of parental loss on the young. So her interest is not so unusual."

"She did say she was looking for patterns of behavior and is working on a research project," says Anita.

Curtis adds, "I have heard her talking about her book writing. I know she and Lucinda have intense conversations about children who lose a parent or parents."

"Lucinda has some pretty strong feelings about the effects of a father abandoning his children. Sharon seems to have similar experiences and feelings with poor parenting. That is the reason they are both great advocates for a particular portion of the population," adds Brooksie.

The three talk about the investigation and their concerns for the safety of group members, both past and present.

The party is over for another year, a party of co-workers and friends, but there is definitely a cloud hanging over everyone's head.

David and Rolland finish their self-appointed job of cleaning. The three of them share a last cup of coffee with Bailey's. Brooksie gives David and Rolland a short version of the possible murders of ex-clients and the ongoing investigation. She thanks them repeatedly for all of their wonderful help, for their friendship, and then say their good nights. *How can I be so fortunate to live next door to such terrific guys. What a priceless gift to have such neighbors.*

CHAPTER XVIII

*Losses that don't get worked through tend to raise their
ugly heads at the most inopportune time.*

Session Nine
BURIED FEELINGS

Kathy and Heidi walk into group arm in arm. Some situational and perhaps, long term friendships are developing within this group. This often happens. People tend to bond, at least for awhile, with those who have had similar traumas.

Their sense of aloneness is temporarily reduced to a tolerable level. They find understanding for a time, because they are sharing a common path and goal.

Justin begins speaking almost before sitting down, "My Shirley has actually asked me to go to the father and daughter picnic. I just hope I don't embarrass her. I'm not very good at playing games and whatever else is done at a picnic."

Harvey tells him to just loosen up and even be silly, have fun.

"Sounds like your daughter is reaching out to you, so whatever you did lately is giving her confidence that you listen and care about her feelings," Rachael offers.

"I am having a little problem with my daughter and my neighbor," says Dell. "One of my neighbors, a single woman, has been bringing dinner over for us the past two weekends. First and second time was much appreciated, but this last weekend she was rather pushy. Cherish was rude to her. I am not in the least bit interested in Mrs. Roke, but I wonder if Cherish is a little jealous. She acts rather possessive of me. What will happen if someday I actually want to date?"

Marshall adds, "Well, I probably shouldn't be the one to give advice, but it sounds like Cherish is just acting like a normal young girl who has lost her mother and still needs reassurance that her father isn't going to leave her, too."

"Sounds like an insightful observation to me, Marshall. Dell can definitely relate to the insecure feelings of Cherish. She will probably continue to adjust to having one parent. Hopefully, she will become more involved with school activities and friends as she gets older," says Rachael.

Brooksie joins in, "When the day comes that you do meet someone you want to date, be honest with Cherish about your feelings and reassure her that no one can replace her mother. Growth is about forward movement. Honesty will be very important. You may want to give her a chance to join a grief support group for children who have lost a parent. I'm sure this issue comes up in those groups frequently."

A lively discussion ensues about the difficulty in sharing hidden, and often embarrassing, thoughts and feelings with family and friends.

Justin shares that he is finding it easier to talk about private stuff with his kids. "Some things I share with my son, and other stuff with my daughters."

"It is easier for me to talk about my anger than about my kinder feelings," says Heidi. "I think I have been angry for many years and I have just been pretending everything is okay in my life.

"When I was a little girl, I had a dog that I loved ferociously. We were best friends. We played together every day, and he slept on my bed every night. One day he was hit and killed by a car. My parents shamed me for crying. They said that an animal had no soul and could easily be replaced. I would have to hold in my tears all day until I went to bed at night. Then, I would cover my head with my pillow and cry myself to sleep."

Another discussion follows, with most of the members telling about the pets they had loved and lost. Several tell about similar experiences to those Heidi had talked about.

The session comes to an end with everyone enjoying a piece of pie that Mary baked.

CHAPTER XIX

Love can outlast pain.

INVESTIGATION CONTINUES

Melissa gives Brooksie a message from Detective Marino, asking her to call him back.

Brooksie dials the phone, "Hello, may I speak to Detective Marino?"

"Hello, detective, I'm returning your call," *Wish I had a more inviting voice. What the heck, I don't have such a voice, don't even know what an inviting voice sounds like. I hate how I stutter, my face feels beat red whenever I have anything to do with Marino. Damn it, I feel like I'm back in high school, acting goofy.*

"I need to talk to you about Lucinda and others. We need more background information on a few of your staff members. Do you do background checks on any of the staff?" responds Marino.

"Melissa is my only employee," says Brooksie. "Yes, I have done a background check on her. I also did background checks on the volunteers. I charge the social workers and the psychologists rent, so they are not employees, and, no, I have not done background checks on them. I obtained a copy of each one's license before I rented to them. Individually, they keep their own financial and client records, except for the support groups. One facilitator in each group is assigned to keep attendance and make notes on progress or concerns of each member. The psychologists are completely separate, having their own waiting area and a different entry and exit door. They take care of their own bookkeeping. Melissa makes appointments for them, answers their phones when they are in session, and sometimes makes photocopies for them. She is a gopher for all of us.

"As far as the rest of the staff, I contact the License Board if there are any past or pending complaints on the social workers, but I did not pay for background checks. Everyone has an updated license which is kept visible in each individual office. Over the last four years, I have gotten to hear some of their personal stories, usually at our social get-togethers. I have a party for everybody, at my home, once or twice a year. It helps us to become more acquainted with each other on a more relaxed and personal level. We are a family of co-workers; a professional family, if you like."

Detective Marino asks, "Would you be comfortable sharing a little of what you know about everyone's personal life with me and Detective Swain? I do understand the confidentiality issue."

"I'm getting a terrible feeling, in my gut, that you are considering some of the staff as suspects. Please, tell me I'm wrong."

"We are trying to solve two murders here. The perpetrator has covered his or her tracks very well. We have darn little to go on and need cooperation and brain storming. We are not accusing anyone, just trying to gather evidence in order to stop any further tragedies. Swain and I would like to ask you a few more questions. It would be better if you are away from the office. Would you be able to come down to the station, or better yet, meet us at the Table Top coffee shop? Say in about one hour from now?" asks Marino.

"I'm not trying to be difficult. I know you are doing your job trying to solve these homicides. It's just that we are close like family at the clinic. I feel uncomfortable talking about my colleagues and friends, behind their backs. Also it is frightening to think you are looking so closely at any one of the staff. I'll be at the coffee shop in an hour."

An hour later the three are sitting in the back booth of Table Top. They all order coffee. Swain asks if she minds that the conversation will be recorded. "Our memories leave a lot to be desired, that is the reason we want to tape the information you share with us." Marino assures her that no one, but the two of them will listen to the tape, and after taking some notes, the tape will be destroyed.

Brooksie nods agreement and starts right in by talking about Melissa.

"Like I said, her main job is to answer the phone, answer questions, schedule appointments for me and for others, staff and clients included. She is the smiling and compassionate face clients first see.

"On the personal side, Melissa is in her early thirties. She has a boyfriend, actually she has several. She loves to have fun. She is quite the flirt. She has a lot of hobbies, but I think her favorites are dancing, dating, beach parties, swimming, and shopping. Even though she has her own apartment, I think she spends a great deal of time at her mother's house. She is a wonderful employee, reliable, conscientious, and always pleasant.

"Detective, you and Detective Swain have already interviewed the staff. What sort of information are you looking for in addition to what you have already been told?" Brooksie asks, while trying to get a look at Marino's left hand. She doesn't spot any ring.

Marino says, "Whatever comes to your mind on the personal side, will be helpful."

Brooksie begins, "I will try to give you a brief overview of each one. Rachael worked one year in Ohio and four years here with me. Her mother died when she was ten or eleven. She was raised by her dad, and complains she had the stepmother from hell. Seldom talks about any guys in her life, except for Richard Adams, an ex-boyfriend, whom she needs to tell you about. He sounds unpredictable and angry. She has told me that she will let you know all about him, when she turns in the information your office has requested from everyone. She has a few girlfriends who she swims with weekly. She is an excellent support group facilitator and an excellent advocate for abused children.

"Lucinda has worked in New York and California and came to my office three years ago. She has been divorced twice. She takes care of her mother, who is seventy and very demanding, calls her at the office many times every day.

"I have been around Lucinda and her mother on numerous occasions, and Mrs. Reicht constantly complains, whines, and belittles Lucinda every chance she gets. I can barely stand to be around her mother for a minute, let alone a lifetime. That mother is every daughter's nightmare. Actually, I could strangle that nasty woman every time I'm in her company and she starts to pick on Lucinda. Guess I shouldn't be saying that sort of thing to the police. Lucinda seems to crumple under her mother's abusiveness.

"Lucinda is an excellent social worker, very organized, conscientious, and compassionate. Her only flaw, that I can see, is the way she lets her mother treat her. I can definitely see why the dad left and why the brothers stay away. Still, it is hard to find an excuse for any dad that leaves his kids, especially with such a selfish and mean person like her mother.

"Am I giving you too many details?" Brooksie asks.

"Not at all. We appreciate your thoroughness."

Brooksie continues talking, "Dan is in his late forties, married ten years to his present wife. He has been a therapist for fourteen years. He sees more male clients than females. Some of his practice is working with probationers. He used to be a dance instructor. That is how he worked his way through college. He loves the women. I think he flirts in his dreams. He obviously has a crush on Lucinda, but I believe he is all talk and no show. Lucinda agrees with me. He may fantasize about being a Casanova, but, in reality, he is quite content just being the protector of this all- female staff.

"He is also an excellent facilitator in the groups and an asset to the clinic, in my opinion.

"I did background checks on Anita and Virginia because they are volunteers and, unlike the social workers, who must carry their own malpractice insurance, I have to carry insurance on them.

"Anita shared her personal history with several of us, over time. She is twenty-five, single, has a brother age twenty-two. Their childhood was lousy. They were both placed in separate foster homes for a short time until their aunt took them in. Anita was sixteen and her brother was thirteen when their mother died of cancer. Anita eventually moved into her own little place. The brother joined the service, but got into drugs. Anita somehow got him help and he straightened out. He is apparently doing well and likes the service, not sure if he is still in. He often stays with Anita. They seem to be very close.

"Anita is quite serious most of the time, always the professional. Recently she has returned to school, she attends at night. She has finished one year and says her goal is to be a psychologist. She and Sharon Primm seem to be rather tight. I wouldn't be surprised if Sharon wasn't helping her financially and doing some mentoring of her.

"Perhaps I should have told you this much earlier, but it didn't seem very significant at the time. Anita told me one time, when her brother was on leave and at home, Jim Marcus showed up at the house and was rather insistent that Anita have coffee with him. Brad escorted him to his car.

"Brad told Anita about two months later, when he was in town, he saw Marcus again, with some woman at a restaurant."

"I'll make a note of that and figure when and how to get with Brad. Maybe he can describe the lady and exactly when he saw them," says Marino.

"Virginia is in her forties. She became a volunteer in the support groups to help herself deal with her own grief. Virginia has three living children, buried a daughter four years ago, the result of a car accident. She is very reliable, a good listener in groups. Listening is a most important trait of a good facilitator.

"The background checks on all three came up spotless.

"Now about me. I've been a social worker for five years. I inherited a home, and this office from a deceased distant relative. My brother died at age twenty-three in a car accident. My father killed himself with a gun when I was thirteen. The same year my brother died. My mother died recently. She had Alzheimers for many years. I have never been married, have no children except for four dogs and six cats, maybe more if my aunt has made an uninvited visit to my house today."

Detective Swain turns off the recorder and asks, "Do you have a boyfriend?"

Brooksie looks directly at Swain, at the same time doing her best to avoid Marino's eyes. She could feel her face getting hot. She knew her cheeks would turn red as a ripe tomato, so in desperation she focuses her undivided attention on her shoes, and quickly says, "No, I haven't much time for a social life, with the exceptions of my so-called dates with my gay neighbors and outings with my office mates."

"Well it seems you and Marino both devote too much time to work and not enough to play. Marino, you don't have a girlfriend either, do you?" asks Swain.

Marino chokes on his coffee, "Went down the wrong tube," Marino blurts out. "No time for dating now, but maybe that will change in the future."

Detective Marino asks, "Do you have any gut feelings about anyone in the office? Anyone seem to be, let's say, acting out of character lately?"

"I have been doing a lot of thinking lately about the staff and just can't imagine anyone of them, and of course that includes me, who seem like they could harm anyone. We are in a helping profession, not a hurting one.

"My concern is growing for two of the men in my group. My concern is for Dell and Justin presently in one of the support groups. They have similar circumstances to the two murdered men. They are both fairly young, wives recently dead, and devoted to young daughters. The other two had young daughters, the fathers started dating, and both daughters had been seeing a therapist to help with dealing with their feelings. Whamo! Both men die. Supposedly, they had been dating a woman who never met the family. Why didn't the daughters meet the woman? That seems so odd, considering what attentive fathers they had been, while they were in the grief groups."

Brooksie takes a long breath and makes eye contact with Marino. He is smiling at her. She makes an attempt to smile back, but it came off more like a twitch. *Now, he probably is thinking I have some horrible kind of physical impairment.*

"Am I getting way off base and letting my imagination go wild?"

"No, you are doing just fine," responds Swain. "I do want to reassure you that we are not only looking for a staff member who might have some connection, because there are others that could have motives and opportunities. The motive is a major puzzler. Hope to have some answers soon, but we really need a break, a lead to follow."

Brooksie says, "In my day planner I wrote on the date Sorensen died. Playing tennis with Rachael for two hours and in the afternoon I was volunteering with my aunt, at the animal shelter. I didn't write down anything the day Marcus died."

"Thanks for your information. If we have any more questions we will get back in touch with you and other staff members. Thanks again," says Marino.

CHAPTER XX

Above all, be patient as I mend. Each celebration reminds
me of other times. I may need four seasons or more,
before I find peace. Each day brings me closer to triumph
over death. Please let me grieve in my own way.

NAN ZASTROW
BLESSED ARE THEY THAT MOURN

SESSION TEN
SPECIAL DATES

Rachael begins the group session, "As some of you have already discovered, certain dates, places, even certain smells can bring on a wave of strong feelings. A few of you have already had the first anniversary of the death of your partner. There will be birthdays, anniversaries, and special events, such as the birth of a child, or grandchild, graduation, other deaths, weddings, divorces, and so forth. So, today let's focus on dates that are and will be special to you in the future."

Kathy speaks first, "Well, I want to share a very special date with all of you. The date is only an estimate, but it will be a date never to be forgotten by me. I am pregnant, almost three and one half months. Thanks, Brooksie, for insisting I see a doctor. Did you suspect?"

"Yes, I did and I was hoping you would be happy if the test was positive."

The room erupted in cheers, clapping, and hugs all around.

You would have thought that they personally were to become a parent.

"I am beyond happy. I feel I have been given a gift from heaven, a gift from my husband. My child is going to know his or her father, with all of the pictures I have of him and all my memories to share with my child."

Dell was first to offer personal congratulations. "How fantastic! A new life is beginning. We are seeing firsthand the circle of life, death, grief, birth, and joy, but not always in that order. I wake up most mornings now, looking forward to the day's activities. I can hardly believe I feel so differently today compared to two months ago. Kathy, I feel like I am sort of becoming an uncle. I am thrilled for you."

"I'm more hopeful too," Heidi says. "My anger, although not completely gone, has certainly lessened. I also feel like a distant relative to your baby, Kathy."

"You don't have to be a distant relative. You can be family! You're the aunt, Heidi. I always wanted a sister."

Marshall quietly asks, "How would you feel about having a gay uncle for your child?"

"Honored and thrilled. I want my child to grow up without crippling prejudices. One more feeling I want to share with all of you is that I no longer have the overpowering desire to go, when the killer has his day in court. I don't want my unborn child to ever feel such terrible hate from his or her own mother. I am going to leave the courts alone to do their job and pray that justice will be fair and swift."

Everyone continues to share meaningful dates. The news of the pregnancy has lightened everyone's mood. There were smiling faces in the circle, unlike previous weeks. New life brings hope.

Brooksie announces since there are only two more sessions to go, the time left will be concentrated on identifying each individual's support system.

Justin gazes around the group. "I hate to bring this up, after such happy and life affirming news for Kathy, but I have some concerns about safety for Dell and even for me. It is our understanding that the two men who were clients at this clinic were also widowers with young daughters. Is there any chance that this clinic or widowers in general are being targeted?"

"That is a very reasonable question, Justin. I'm sorry I didn't bring it up sooner. After our session next week, the detectives are going to be here to answer our questions. In the meantime, they have asked us to be alert to anything we feel uncomfortable about. If at any time anyone of you has a concern, no matter how insignificant you think it is, please call the detectives. I am handing out phone numbers that they gave to me. You can call at any time, day or night."

As the group breaks up, Kathy receives more hugs and well wishes. The laughter was music to the ears of Rachael, Anita, and Brooksie.

De-briefing session

Anita, Rachael, and Brooksie have just started, when Lucinda and Virginia come into the room. They ask if everyone could go out for a bite to eat and talk about what was going on.

After settling into a comfortable booth, at Table Top Café, Anita informs her companions that her brother has seen a woman recently, in the office parking lot, the same one he had seen with Jim Marcus some time ago. We agree the detectives need to speak with Brad.

Brooksie pulls out her cell phone and calls the department. Detective Swain returns the call a few minutes later. Anita takes the phone and tells the detective that her brother had seen a lady with Jim Marcus and has seen her again lately, in the office parking lot.

The detective asks Anita if she could have Brad come to the

department and give a description to their artist. Anita agrees and after hanging up from Swain, she immediately calls her brother with the detective's request.

Brad answers the phone and tells his sister, "I have another commitment today. I will go tomorrow afternoon. You want to go with me, Anita?"

"Sure. See you later tonight."

CHAPTER XXI

*The experiences of life are important only in
the attitudes we form about them.*

AUTHOR UNKNOWN

PREDATORS AND PREY

Marino and Swain are both busily going over their notes. Marino says, "I have finally reached Rachael's ex-boyfriend, Richard Adams. He isn't too happy about my telling him he needs to come in today to answer a few questions. He got pretty ugly on the phone, but calmed down immediately when I suggested I send a police car to bring him in or would he prefer to make his own transportation arrangements. He is due here shortly."

Moments later, an unkempt, body-builder looking guy, approaches Marino's desk.

"The guy up front says you're Marino. So here I am. Now what's so damn important I have to drop everything and race down here?'

Marino says, "You must be Richard Adams. Thanks for coming in so quickly. Have a seat. My partner and I have a few questions." Marino gives Richard the dates of the homicides and asks him if he can remember his whereabouts on those dates.

"I know they were awhile back. Maybe we can give you some time, say a week or so, to try to figure out where you were at the times we are asking about."

"You gotta be kidding. Like I know where I was a year ago. I do happen to know about six months ago, 'cause I was in the hospital for surgery and I can prove it. Why do you guys want to know where I was at those times?"

Swain says, "Did you know a Jim Marcus or a Ray Sorensen? They both had been enrolled in grief groups. Where your ex-girlfriend, Rachael, works. Both men have had an unnatural death."

"I get it. Rachael has been telling you things about me so now I'm a suspect? She is such a lying bitch. When I first met up with her, I thought she was great. As time went by, she started the lying about her relationships with other men. I think she was messing around with clients. Maybe you need to take a real close look at her. She is quite an actress, but down deep she really hates men, especially her dad. She cheated on me every chance she could."

"Please give us the name of the hospital, your doctor and the exact dates you were a patient? You can call us or come back in with the information. Also try to figure out where you were the year before on the date of Mr. Marcus's death. I would suggest you do this as soon as possible, then we won't have to bother you anymore," says Swain.

Detective Moreno adds, "I strongly suggest you do not try to communicate with Rachael, either by phone, mail or in person. We will take any and all threats to her very seriously. Do you understand?"

"I get your message. I'll call back here when I can figure out where I was last year in June. Are we finished here?"

After Richard leaves, Marino asks Swain to make the call to verify the hospital dates. "I can't imagine Rachael dating such a jerk. I will call and let her know we interviewed him. I plan to tell her to keep a sharp lookout for Richard and to add we have warned him to have no contact with her. That guy is trouble, but if his alibi is good we can probably eliminate him, at least for Sorensen's death."

The next day, Brad and Anita show up for the appointment

at the police department, to see the artist. They are ushered into a small office and introduced to Ms. Summers. "Together Brad, you and I, are going to come up with a drawing of what you remember of a certain lady. I understand you saw her about a year ago and again in the last month or so."

"Yes I sure hope I can remember enough of how she looked," Brad answers nervously.

Ms. Summers says, "Let's begin and remember there is no pass or fail, so no reason to be nervous. Was her face round or long?"

Brad sitting by the artist's side answers questions as to what different parts of the face looked like. It is slow work, but as the time passes, a face starts to appear on her drawing pad.

"What color was her hair?" asks Ms. Summers.

"I'm not sure. I sort of remember two different colors. The first time I saw her she looked like a brunette, but the second time her hair was much lighter. She was wearing a hat that time, I can't be sure of the color. Sorry, wish I could be more exact."

A little later the artist says, "The sketch is finished. You did a great job describing this person."

Brad and Anita both look over the lady's shoulder at the drawing.

Brad enthusiastically says, "Your drawing looks like the woman I saw. You are really good at this Ms. Summers."

Anita gasps, "My God that looks a little like Sharon, or maybe Maureen. I've never met Maureen, but I have seen a picture of her. They both have those high cheek bones, chiseled noses, and full lips. I'm sure there are many other women who could fit this picture. I will not believe Sharon could be any part of any homicide."

Brad and Anita leave the police station, Brad drops his sister off at the clinic and he heads home.

Anita is met at the door by Brooksie and Rachael. At first

glance they could both see that Anita looks upset. They usher her into Brooksie's office and offer her some water.

"How did it go with Brad and the drawing?" Rachael asks.

Anita, visibly pale, says, "The artist drew a picture that looks a little like Sharon or her sister, actually, it looked a lot like one of them. There must be some kind of mistake. Sharon is so good to me. She is caring, never seems to tire of helping others. I'm aware of the fact sometimes she seems standoffish, but I know what a big heart she possess. No one can ever make me believe she is capable of killing those two clients. My God, she is like a mother, sister, mentor, and friend to me, constantly encouraging me to do my best. What do you suppose the detectives are going to do now, once they have seen that picture? What am I going to say to Sharon?"

Brooksie answers, "I have no idea. We will have to wait and see what Marino and Swain tell us. Sharon is your friend, so talk to her like a friend. See what she says and how she reacts. I agree with you, Anita. Sharon is one very devoted psychologist and is always hard at work assisting others to improve their lives. Integrity flows through her pores. I can't see her harming any soul."

"I agree with you both. There must be many who can fit Brad's description," adds Rachael. "In fact, I can easily suspect my ex-boyfriend. Maybe he has hooked up with a woman who looks like Sharon, and she has become his accomplice. He is unpredictable, mean and could lie to God. I think he is capable of murder. The detectives even told me to be observant and to call them if he causes me any problems. I'm thinking of buying a gun to keep by my bed."

"Rachael, stay with me if you feel there is even a tiny chance of problems with Richard."

"Thanks Brooksie, I will if Richard threatens me."

CHAPTER XXII

Grieving is hard. It need not be hellish.

ALLA RENEE BOZARTH, PH.D.
LIFE IS GOODBYE, LIFE IS HELLO

SESSION ELEVEN
HONOR THE PAST
AND EMBRACE THE PRESENT

"We have one more session after today," says Brooksie. "I'm sorry to say that Anita won't be with us today. She called in sick. Right now, I want each one of you to identify your own personal support system. Who are you going to talk with when times get tough? What steps will you take to get help for yourself when you know you need some outside help?"

Kathy immediately identifies each member of the group as the greatest support system she had ever known. She also feels there will be helpful support coming from the church that she attends infrequently. "My mother-in-law has made herself readily available to me, and I'm grateful for her comfort."

Justin speaks next, "My children are my best support." I hope to remain in the lives of this group, especially with the men. I have not really had close men friends in the past, and I believe I have been missing out. Not to exclude you wonderful ladies. Kathy, you truly helped to open my eyes to the myth that showing emotion is unprofessional. I, too, would like to be one of your child's uncles, if you would allow me that honor."

"You're on."

Heidi smiles. "Support for me will be this group, a few special friends, and, of course, the clinic's staff."

Dell says his daughter, mother, this group and staff, plus a few of his co-workers and boss will all be part of his support system.

Marshall joins in, "Never thought I could become so accepted with a group of 'straights', and I'm so comfortable with each one of you. I had a lovely dream last night. I was walking in some kind of field and coming toward me was a truck, but when it got closer it looked more like a float. The kind of float you would see in a parade. It stopped in front of me and a person beckoned me to get on board. There were several kinds of animals, friendly ones, already on board. I was trying to get on board when I woke up. I still feel at peace because of that dream."

Mary adds, "I am so surprised how differently I feel today compared to just short of three months ago. It feels strange to me that I feel so close to all of you who were strangers just eleven weeks ago. My support will come from all of you, family, and a few co-workers. This may sound silly, but, when I am at loose ends, I can bake something, anything and feel at peace."

A few join in and agree maybe they should learn to bake as well.

Harvey continues the assignment by saying his son is his number one support, plus, of course, this group. "I have the same sentiments that Justin shared. I've not had many real close male friends. I did when I was a boy, but somehow my job took so much of my time. Then, when Helen and I married, she became my constant companion, my support system, and I hers."

Justin adds, with a twinkle in his eye, "My widower status has recently become a topic of discussion among the secretaries and nurses. A few of my patients, or the mothers of patients, plus a nurse or two, have been paying a great deal of attention to me. There are offers of home cooked meals and invitations to events.

"Most embarrassing is my own behavior. I have been acting

like a pimply faced teenager to the point of getting flushed and stuttering. I feel like I'm back in high school and standing nervously with my buddies against the gym wall at a school dance.

"I have a mix of emotions, flattered and repulsed at the same time. I still feel very married. The best part is that I can laugh at myself and my own discomfort."

A brief discussion follows about the tendency as time goes by to make the departed one into a saint and, less often, to remember their not so endearing habits and traits.

Most expressed a worry about feeling a sense of betraying their loved one, if they were to ever be in another romantic relationship.

Mary ends the session with, "There is a reason for the words, 'Until death do us part.' I think it would be a betrayal of myself if I shut myself in and never considered opening up to new relationships, romantic or otherwise."

At the end of the session they talk about the ongoing investigation. Dell and Justin have been talking with the detectives. They have been told to let the detectives know if anything, at all, seemingly unusual happens to them. They have been instructed to be cautious if they are approached by strangers. The group express, in unison, best wishes for a speedy recovery for Anita. The members disperse with the exception of Rachael and Brooksie.

"I hope it is nothing serious for Anita," says Rachael. "I wonder if Brad's description he gave to the police artist identified a specific person?"

Brooksie replies, "Anita didn't sound like herself. Thought she might be coming down with the flu and thought it better if she stayed home.   I am confident the members have all figured out reasonable support systems for themselves. In my opinion, all have made progress and feel more in control of their lives. What's your impression, Rachael?"

"I think they are all amazing. They are reminding me why I love to facilitate a grief group. It is like watching the determination and perseverance of a blade of grass that, despite all odds, will stick its tiny face up through the concrete or asphalt street. There is no stopping the spirit of life."

CHAPTER XXIII

*"Time itself doesn't heal. It only gives us room to free ourselves,
and the opportunity to heal ourselves of past wounds."*

ALLA RENEE BOZARTH, PH.D,
LIFE IS GOODBYE, LIFE IS HELLO

POLICE STATION

Detective Marino is talking with Swain. "I've called Sharon Primm and set up an appointment with her and her sister for tomorrow. She asked if she could come in today, in the late afternoon, and speak with us. I told her 5 o'clock would be fine. I have an uneasy feeling about that lady. I'm going to send someone to watch her house today through tomorrow. That rendering by Ms. Summers, of Brad's description, sure as hell looks like Sharon or someone very much like her. It also looks a great deal like the sketch of what the ranger lady remembered.

Sharon arrives and is shown a seat. "I understand that Brad has seen a woman with Jim Marcus and that you had him describe her to the department's artist. I have brought a picture of myself and Maureen. Would you tell me if there is any resemblance to the police drawing?"

Marino responds, "Do you want to look at the sketch?"

"Yes. I would appreciate that."

Swain goes to the file and brings back the drawing and places it in front of Sharon.

She stares at it for a long minute. "Thank you for your courtesy. My sister and I have an appointment for tomorrow and

I won't forget." Sharon gracefully walks slowly out of the station and gets into her car, drives away.

Detective Swain says, "Did you see how white she turned when she saw the drawing. I thought she might faint. She acted cool as a cucumber, but her lack of color told a different story."

"We have her statement as to where she was on the dates in question, her alibis have checked out. She wasn't even in the state either time. We don't know much about her sister. She has been difficult to get hold of. I get the feeling Sharon runs interference for her. Maybe it is just a case of over protection for 'baby' sister. Whatever, the case I plan to keep them both in my sights. Like I said before, my gut is talking loud and clear. Sharon and Maureen's houses are under surveillance starting today. I want to know where they both are day and night. I don't think this is going to end well."

CHAPTER XXIV

Life is real! Life is earnest! And the grave is not its goal; Dust
thou art, to dust returnest, was not spoken of the soul.

HENRY WADSWORTH LONGFELLOW

SESSION TWELVE
ENDINGS AND BEGINNINGS

A surprise shower for Kathy has been put together by the group members for this last session. Not only is Kathy surprised, but Rachael, Anita, and Brooksie have also been kept in the dark. This is going to be an unusual last session, but it feels appropriate and heart-warming. Brooksie thinks to herself as she watches each one come into the room, *I'm awe-struck by how differently they look and carry themselves today compared to the first time they came into this room. There is lightness to their steps, and more aliveness in their voices. Their grooming is improved, the dark circles are not so prominent and most noticeable, all are smiling. God I love this work.*

"Personally, I must admit I have a lump in my throat. I don't like endings near as well as I like the beginnings," Rachael shares.

Heidi says, "I have mixed emotions. Not too sure about my future. I never thought I could survive the death of my loved one. But I am, and each day that passes I feel stronger, or more confident, in my own abilities."

"We don't get to pick our family, but we do have choices when it comes to friends," says Mary.

Justin stands up and announces, "I wish to say goodbye for

now, by doing something this group has taught me to do. I want to hug everyone in this room and I will let my hugs express my feelings. I need to practice on willing volunteers. You folks are the ones."

All stand up while Justin makes his "practice" rounds.

Brooksie starts in, "You have all been courageous and have worked hard in these sessions. This last session is always rather bittersweet for me. It has been an honor accompanying all of you on this painful and life-changing journey. Some days, you may need to back track for a short time, and that's okay, just don't spend a lot of time retracing your steps."

Rachael also thanks the members for allowing her to briefly share in their unique lives, and reminds them to call the clinic any time they feel they need a little boost of encouragement or a listening ear.

Marshall and Harvey both express their gratitude and new sense of hope.

Next, as a group, they walk Kathy over to the corner of the room, where a large unknown something is covered by a huge sheet. Kathy is asked to remove the sheet. She does so and gasps when she sees a beautiful crib filled to capacity with baby clothes, diapers, pictures frames, photo album for First Baby, and many other items for a newborn. Each member had placed an I.O.U. in an envelope stating: for one free night of babysitting.

Kathy's eyes fill to running over. The room erupts with laughter, tears, words of wisdom from the experienced parents, for a new parent, and a great deal of joy and hope for all. Everyone takes their turn and time saying goodbye to each and all. Promises are made to stay in touch. The group agrees on a date to meet in one month at a nearby restaurant. Rachael, Anita, and, Brooksie are included in the invitation.

The three staff members remain to clean up, after the others have left the room.

"You don't seem to be yourself, Anita. Is something wrong, something worrying you?" asks Brooksie.

"I don't know if I'm supposed to say anything, but if I don't I feel like I may explode. I've just got to tell someone. You know that Brad gave a description to the police's artist, of the woman he saw with Mr. Marcus and then he saw her again in our parking lot recently?"

"Yes you did tell us that," says Rachael.

Anita takes a deep breath and in a barely heard whisper says, "It looked like Sharon or at least someone with her great features. I will never believe in a million years Sharon could have murdered those men. Never, never can anyone convince me of that."

"What did the detectives say to you about the resemblance?" asks Brooksie.

"Nothing, they only thanked Brad for his help and said they would be in touch."

Rachael offers, "Maybe we three could drive down to the station and ask the detectives what is happening with the investigation, later today?"

"We could do that or we can just wait for the detectives to tell us what they want us to know. Anita, there are many females who look similar to Sharon. Half of the movie stars, on TV and in the movies, have her high cheek bones and flawless skin. We don't know for sure that a woman is the killer, could be a man. I know how much you think of Sharon. No way can I imagine her as a homicidal maniac," responds Brooksie.

CHAPTER XXV

One who has journeyed in a strange land cannot return unchanged.

C.S. LEWIS

A WEEK LATER

Brooksie arrives early at the office. She is doing paper work for the next support group that is to begin tomorrow. This group will be a divorce group. The clients turn in short applications and are assigned an interview with a social worker. This is done to try to choose appropriate individuals for each group. Time passes by slowly, as a much distracted Brooksie dreads a phone call from the detectives. The room was as silent as a cemetery at midnight.

The phone rings, sounding more like tornado alert to Brooksie's ears. It is Sharon.

"Brooksie, I need for you and Anita to come to my house as quickly as possible. You are a good friend to Anita and she is going to need you. I have something I must say. Please, come now, just the two of you. I'll explain when you get here."

Brooksie thinking to herself, *Sharon's voice sounds hollow, with little inflection, I have never heard her say please before. She sounds almost like she is pleading.*

Brookie quickly dials Anita's home, her hands are shaking. When Anita answers she tells her about Sharon's request and asks her to meet her at Sharon's house. "It will take us both about fifteen minutes to get there. Wait outside her house if you get there first, we can go in together,"

Brooksie races out of the office, grabs her cell phone and makes a beeline for Sharon's place, with enough adrenalin flowing through her to fuel an Amtrak train. Brooksie arrives first soon followed by Anita.

Anita drives up, parks next to Brooksie, runs, jumps into the passenger side, and says, "What is going on? What could Sharon possibly want to tell us? I can feel my heart pumping so hard I can see my shirt move to each beat.

"I'm without a clue, Anita, just like you. Sharon didn't sound like herself on the phone. Whatever she has to say, she wants you to have a friend nearby, for some reason. Let's go."

Before they could open the car doors, a tall man, looking like he'd forgotten to shave that morning asks them where they were going. He identifies himself as Officer Johnson and shows them his identification. He explains that Sharon's house has been under surveillance for a time. Brooksie hurriedly explains the phone call from Sharon. Anita starts to tear up, tiny drops of moisture landing on her skirt. The officer asks them to remain in the car, while he places a call to the detectives.

Marino answers the call, "Have the ladies wait until we can get there. It will take us about twenty minutes, maybe less with the siren blasting."

Swain and Marino pull in behind Anita's car, after a time. Brooksie repeats to the detectives Sharon's request. Marino sends the officer to the back of the house.

Detective Swain is furtively looking through a window. He reports back, "Sharon is sitting on the couch and looks like her sister is asleep, next to her."

Marino tells Brooksie and Anita to go to the front door and knock, and that he and Swain will be next to them, but out of sight. "When you enter, do not close the door tightly," says Marino. "By the way, Sharon is not a suspect, but we have had our team looking at Maureen.

The women walk up to the door and knock gently. A muted voice answers, "The door is unlocked, come in."

Brooksie and Anita enter slowly, waiting for their eyes to adjust to the dimness in the room. Sharon is sitting on the couch, with Maureen stretched out lengthwise on the sofa, her head resting in her sister's lap. Maureen appears to be sleeping. Sharon's eyes appear to blank and sad, at the same time. She is gently stroking her sister's long red hair.

"She can no longer hurt herself or anyone else," Sharon whispers. There is mascara running down Sharon's cheeks and her eyes were swollen and moist.

Anita and I stand frozen in the middle of the room.

Sharon speaks, "She is gone."

Anita starts to cry, and Brooksie asks if she could move closer to the couch. Sharon nods affirmatively. Brooksie asks if she can take Maureen's pulse.

"You can, but there is no need. I know she is gone," answers Sharon. "I couldn't let her kill another one."

Brooksie slowly approaches the couch and places her fingers on Maureen's wrist. No pulse is detected and no visible chest movements.

At this time, the detectives quietly come into the room. Sharon briefly looks up at them, makes no comment, simply continues to strokes her sister's lifeless forehead..

"When did you first suspect your sister of the killings?" asks Brooksie.

"When I told Maureen that Anita's brother had seen Jim Marcus with a woman on two occasions and that he was meeting at the police station to give a description to the police artist. Then, I knew.

"She started acting strange, even stranger than usual. She had always been quick to anger, especially if she didn't get her own way. Maureen yelled out, 'No one can identify someone from a sketch, after they have only seen a person for a minute, in the mall.' She got loud and angry with me and said she had told me not to get so close to Anita. She told me that Anita has been using me all along and that she never did trust her. She even accused Anita of being jealous of her.

"The more hysterical Maureen became, the more I started to panic. I had not said anything about a mall. How would she know about that?

"My sister has been on and off medications for the last five years. I have dragged her to several psychiatrists and a few psychologists, but she would only go a few times. She would make up all kinds of excuses and even lie about their inappropriate behaviors. She would say that the male therapists had come on to her. One psychiatrist in particular, whom I have known for years and who I happen to know is gay, told me that Maureen was acting very seductive. She even continued to try to seduce him after he informed her about his sexual orientation. He told me he wasn't willing to work with her and gave me other referrals. It went that way with all of the referrals, even the women psychologist and psychiatrist. If she couldn't seduce them, she would say they threatened her.

"I have known for a long time that she was narcissistic, had sociopathic tendencies, displayed poor impulse control, and was obsessive. She had hated men, in general, since she was young. She had been promiscuous since age fourteen, or maybe she was fifteen. I can't remember exactly. She would tell a lie, even if telling the truth would have been of benefit for her.

"I have been suspicious of her since Ray Sorensen's body was discovered. She had been asking me questions about the men clients in the support groups. I keep my research records on some of the clients that attended grief groups for the past several years. They are locked up in my home office and in a locked filing cabinet. Maureen would have been capable of stealing my keys and making duplicates. I believe that is how she knew about Mr.

Sorensen and Mr. Marcus. I feel so terribly responsible for her being able to find out about the widowers.

"Lucinda and Anita both told me that she would ask them about certain male clients and they were getting uncomfortable around her. The day before Mr. Sorensen's death, she told me she had a very special date the following day. I saw her packing a bathing suit and asked her what kind of date? She answered, 'A wet one'. I didn't ask more.

"This morning, I called her and asked her to come to my house, told her I had something very important to discuss with her. When she came in I asked her right up front why Ray Marcus and Jim Sorensen?

"My sister laughed and said, 'They were going to screw up their daughters' lives because they only thought about their own pleasures. They were despicable. I saved their daughters from hell. Now is our little discussion over with? I have plans for today.'

"I knew right then what I needed to do. I could not turn her into the police. I couldn't bear the thought of her spending the rest of her life in prison. She would have only become crazier. She was more like my daughter than a sister. I have taken care of her since she was six years old. She was too dangerous for society and there would be no real treatments for her. There would be no hope of a future for her.

"I asked her to stay for breakfast. She acquiesced with a pouty expression. I made crepes, her favorite, and squeezed oranges for juice. I loaded the juice with Zonact, the very drug I had found in her house a few days ago. I mixed in more of the drug in the filling for the crepes. I knew I was mixing in a lethal dose.

"As she became sleepy and unsteady on her feet, I helped her to the couch. As she slipped away, she looked at me with such a look of confusion and betrayal. I told her I loved her, but she had to be stopped. I held her on my lap until her breathing ceased. I have been waiting for you to arrive. Anita, I wanted you to hear this from my lips. I'm so very sorry that Maureen and I have caused you so much pain and sorrow.

"I am guilty of a mercy killing. I know what I did was wrong in the eyes of the law, but I have no regrets. My sister is no longer living her crazy existence and can no longer harm another."

Anita begins crying in earnest, slides down onto the floor next to Sharon's legs. Sharon pats her tenderly on top of her head.

Detective Swain excuses himself to make a call to his precinct, to summon the coroner.

Detective Marino gently helps Sharon to her feet and reads her rights to her, "I am placing you under arrest for the murder of your sister. Do you understand that anything you say can and will be used against you in a court of law?"

Sharon barely whispers a yes. "Please tell the clinic's staff how very sorry I am for all the pain my sister and I have caused. Anita, please don't let this tragedy become yours. You have a very promising future in front of you. I know you will help many some day."

Later on back at the office building, shock and unbelievable sadness blanket the clinic that day and for many days and weeks that follow.

A day later, Detectives Marino and Swain arrive at the clinic's office along with the rest of the clinic's staff. We all gather in the large group room. Detective Swain hands over a tape that Sharon had previously recorded. Rachael slips it into the machine and all listen, with wet cheeks, to her message: "I was nine years old and Maureen was six years old when mother died of an overdose. Her death was ruled a suicide. The first year after her death, our father was very attentive and did an excellent of job of acting mother and father to us. But there was one very big problem, Dad forbade us to mention our mother, her life or death, and we were punished if we cried or tried to say we missed her. All of our mother's pictures disappeared. Every article of clothing, every shoe, hairbrush, and piece of jewelry was thrown away in the trash. Soon after, Dad started dating some woman and married her. She was practically a stranger to us. We were forbidden to speak about our mother to her. She was a selfish woman and paid absolutely no attention to us. We were neglected, ignored, and when she did speak to us, it was in an angry, disgusted voice. She hated us. I think she probably hated all kids.

"Dad was absent from home more and more, all the time. I was beginning to be the main caregiver for Maureen and myself. About a year or so later, Dad hired some older woman to do all of the house chores, and that included taking care of us two girls. She was also mean, cruel, and lazy. I did more house work than she did.

"Maureen and I shared our bedroom, so I would hear her cry herself to sleep every night until she was about eight or nine. She began to tell me how much she hated our dad, his new wife and the horrible housekeeper. She even told me she wished they would all die. I believe she had begun to fantasize about their deaths. Once in awhile, she would tell me how she would kill them. I told her to stop thinking and talking about such things. She did stop talking to me, but I don't think she stopped thinking about it, not for one minute did she stop. I believe she became obsessed with payback.

"By the time she was eighteen, she was seriously into drugs, sex, drinking, and other risky behaviors.

"My sister is the reason I became a psychologist. My goal has always been to help my damaged sibling. I failed her miserably.

"My beautiful sister used her physical body to pay our Dad back by sleeping with anyone and everyone, and telling dad the details. In her sick mind, she generalized her hate to reach all men, fathers especially, who neglected or in any other way abused their roles.

"Dad denied his own grief when Mom took her own life. When I was older I believed he was so angry with mom because she took her own life and left the three of us. He couldn't get over his rage and that is why he made us get rid of all of her possessions. He didn't allow Maureen or me any natural outlet for our grief. Maureen turned her deepening depression into irrational, obsessive anger.

"I turned my pent up emotions into the activity of studying human behavior. Maureen took one path and I the other. Yet we both have become killers.

"Please, continue to assist the bereaved. My heart aches for the pain that Maureen has caused for many. Anita, I know how much your brother means to you and how much you mean to him. You have been a mother, father, friend, policeman, and therapist for him. Like I have tried to be for my sister. I even took it one step further, and became her executioner. May you never take that role. You mean a great deal to me. I know you will make a great psychologist. I have signed over all my assets to you. Please see Mr. Williams. He is my attorney and has all of the signed paper work. I did that over a week ago. Guess I knew something, without really knowing what, exactly. Please finish school and serve your clients with truth and passion.

"I apologize to all of you for failing to see how dangerous my sister had become. I don't ask for forgiveness, but I do ask for compassion for Maureen and myself. Please help the Marcus and Sorensen families."

When the tape ended, it took quite a while for the sniffling to quiet down. Brad was trying to comfort his sister, but she was inconsolable. He simply held her until her tears dried up.

Detectives Swain and Marino, accompanied by Lucinda, Rachael, Dan and myself, all went to inform the two victims' families about Dr. Primm's involvement and Maureen's guilt.

Brooksie closes the clinic for two weeks. What an emotional rollercoaster for all concerned. Even the Detectives looked like they, too, had been run over by a two ton truck.

Brooksie thinking to herself, *I know in time and with a lot of talking, venting, crying, and sharing we will get back to doing the valuable work of assisting others with their grief. Right now, we need to take care of our own. Hopefully, my next support group won't be so deadly.*

Brooksie adds, "I believe that each staff member will do whatever they can to support Sharon. I for one, will go to the hearings, and do my very best to remain a nonjudgmental friend, for as long as she wants and needs my friendship. I think many of the others will do the same. Anita has already taken steps to let Sharon know she still cares deeply for her and is thankful for the financial help."

Anita tearfully states, "I will graduate with honors to show Sharon her sacrifice will not go unnoticed. She will continue to be my mentor, no matter what the courts decide her new address will be and for how long."

Brooksie is the last one to leave the office and closes up the place for the next few weeks. *I just want to get myself home and sit quietly in my garden with my beloved, uncomplicated and always loving dogs and cats.*

As she heads towards her car, Detective Marino stops her and asks if she would join him for a cup of coffee before heading home.

Well, my darling pets will be just fine for another hour or so. She smiles her Cheshire cat smile, and reaches for his outstretched hand, "My car or yours?"

ABOUT THE AUTHOR

Donna Reutzel Underwood is a registered nurse who has been involved in grief work for twenty years, as a counselor, group facilitator, and as a volunteer. Donna is married to Wayne, mother to Karla and Erik, mother-in-law to Nathan, and grandmother of eight. She has recently discovered her biological family, a sister also named Donna, a brother-in-law Jack, a brother Ronald, deceased, niece, Jody and three nephews, Robert, Lawrence, and Greg plus their children. Donna is a member of Kiwanis, and a volunteer Guardian ad Litem. She lives in Kennewick, Washington with her husband, two dogs and three cats.